Bawdy Bedtime Stories

Bawdy
Bedtime Stories

JOAN ELIZABETH LLOYD

HEAT | NEW YORK

THE BERKLEY PUBLISHING GROUP
Published by the Penguin Group
Penguin Group (USA) Inc.
375 Hudson Street, New York, New York 10014, USA
Penguin Group (Canada), 90 Eglinton Avenue East, Suite 700, Toronto, Ontario M4P 2Y3, Canada
(a division of Pearson Penguin Canada Inc.)
Penguin Books Ltd., 80 Strand, London WC2R 0RL, England
Penguin Group Ireland, 25 St. Stephen's Green, Dublin 2, Ireland (a division of Penguin Books Ltd.)
Penguin Group (Australia), 250 Camberwell Road, Camberwell, Victoria 3124, Australia
(a division of Pearson Australia Group Pty. Ltd.)
Penguin Books India Pvt. Ltd., 11 Community Centre, Panchsheel Park, New Delhi—110 017, India
Penguin Group (NZ), 67 Apollo Drive, Rosedale, North Shore 0632, New Zealand
(a division of Pearson New Zealand Ltd.)
Penguin Books (South Africa) (Pty.) Ltd., 24 Sturdee Avenue, Rosebank, Johannesburg 2196,
South Africa

Penguin Books Ltd., Registered Offices: 80 Strand, London WC2R 0RL, England

This book is an original publication of The Berkley Publishing Group.

This is a work of fiction. Names, characters, places, and incidents either are the product of the author's imagination or are used fictitiously, and any resemblance to actual persons, living or dead, business establishments, events, or locales is entirely coincidental. The publisher does not have any control over and does not assume any responsibility for author or third-party websites or their content.

Copyright © 2008 by Joan Elizabeth Lloyd.
Cover photo by Jupiterimages.
Cover design by Pyrographx.
Text design by Kristin del Rosario.

All rights reserved.
No part of this book may be reproduced, scanned, or distributed in any printed or electronic form without permission. Please do not participate in or encourage piracy of copyrighted materials in violation of the author's rights. Purchase only authorized editions.
HEAT and the HEAT design are trademarks belonging to Penguin Group (USA) Inc.

ISBN-13: 978-0-7394-9532-2

Contents

Introduction

❦

CROTIC TALES TAKE MANY FORMS, FROM DRAMATIC SHORT stories to delightful interludes, and I love them all. An erotic tale can take you into a married couple's bedroom or an elevator in a high-rise. In a fantasy, you can be on a pirate ship or a plane at thirty thousand feet, in a hot tub or a tiny sports car. Erotic stories can transport you to another time or another reality. They are so deliciously personal that most will raise your temperature level, although a few might not. If you begin to read one and it's not your cup of tea, flip the pages to the next tale. There's quite an assortment here.

Fiction can transport you anywhere, but have you ever thought that a sexy tale could be educational? Some of the tales in *Bawdy Bedtime Stories* might have you thinking, "Wow, I'd love to try that position or technique." Then you wonder: What about trying that with my lover? Could he or she be interested? Might your partner want to play like this too?

Don't let that thought escape. Put it, and the erotic tale that triggered it, to use. Expand your horizons. How? Take a little risk. Slip a bookmark into that particularly delicious story and give the book to your partner. Ask him or her to read this Introduction, then read the tale you marked. You might discover that he or she will take the hint and is, indeed, interested. Wow—a new path to follow.

Of course, your partner might not be turned on by the same thing that curls your toes. Okay. If your partner isn't into that activity, maybe he or she will take a little risk and move the bookmark to another story that lights his or her fire. Bravo! You two have begun to communicate. You're both on your way to new fun and games.

Maybe, however, you just want to read and enjoy. That's fine too. In either case, turn the page and have a blast!

A Hot Summer Night

❧

IT WAS PROBABLY THE HOTTEST EVENING OF THE ENTIRE summer, and the Hoffmans' central air-conditioning was on the fritz and had been that way since that morning. Gone. Out. Dead as a doornail. And tonight it was almost literally hot as hell in the house. Sandy Hoffman had called a repairman, but he wouldn't be able to make a house call, as he put it, until the following afternoon.

During the day everything had been fine. Both Sandy and her husband, Brant, had air-conditioning at work, and they'd gone out for dinner and an air-conditioned movie. That morning they'd made arrangements for the kids to have sleepover dates with friends so they'd be cool, but now Sandy and Brant were in the house, contemplating a good night's sleep that just wasn't going to happen.

"We could go to a motel," Sandy suggested.

"That's really extravagant," Brant said, "but we can if you like. However, I've got a silly idea that might just work. It's cooler outside than in here, so why don't we take a few blankets for padding and make a bed out in the yard?"

"Sleep outdoors?" Sandy said immediately. "With the bugs?"

"God, you're such a wimp," Brant said with a chuckle. "We can bring bug spray if you want, but, insects or no insects, it's got to be cooler out there than in here and cheaper than a motel."

Sandy was quiet for a few minutes, then nodded. "I hate to admit it, but I think you've had a good idea." She giggled. "Sleeping outdoors. Who'da thunk it?"

"Let's see what we have to put underneath us so we won't ruin any good bedding." The pair rummaged in the linen closet and found several old blankets that they used at the beach. While Sandy grabbed the sheet from their bed and carried the whole pile downstairs, Brant pulled two cold beers from the fridge and joined her. As they walked out the back door, they both relished the drop in temperature. "This is sooo much better," Sandy admitted. They found a flat spot under a maple tree, spread their makeshift bed and stretched out.

"I have to admit that it's really nice out here," Sandy said, enjoying the feel of the slight breeze that cooled her skin. "I'm starting to get what squirrels see in this outdoor stuff. I wouldn't make a habit of it, of course, but for right now, it's kinda nice."

After a few minutes and several swigs of beer, Brant said, "Why don't you take off that tee shirt and enjoy the air?" He made short work of his.

"You guys have it great. A bare chest is fine for you. Totally decent. Us girls can't just take off our tops."

"Of course you can. No one can see." To distract his wife, he popped the top on her beer and handed her the frosty can.

"Everyone can see. The Haverstraws, the Morgans," she said, mentioning the neighbors on either side of the house. "All they have to do is to glance out their bedroom windows and . . ." She took a long pull of the beer.

"There are no lights out here and we're almost hidden beneath this tree. And anyway, they wouldn't think to look for us out here. Why should they?"

When Sandy became thoughtful, Brant continued. "The cool air feels great on my skin. You really ought to try it."

Sandy was usually pretty conservative about sexual things, but Brant thought he might just convince her to loosen up a little this evening. "It's after ten and," he said, pointing to the downstairs windows in both neighboring houses, "most of their lights are out. Come on. Who's to know? Be a little daring. I know you'll like it."

"Okay," Sandy said. "Here goes." She pulled her tee shirt over her head, revealing her small but inviting breasts.

The light of the half-moon shone on her lovely body, and Brant's thoughts immediately jumped into his shorts. "Stretch out and you'll realize how nice this all feels," he said, sipping his brew.

Sandy lay back on the sheet and wriggled, obviously enjoying the sensuous feel of the soft fabric on her back. "This is entirely too decadent," she purred.

"You could make it even more so," Brant said. "How about the shorts too?"

She gasped. "I couldn't." Then she paused. "Could I?"

Brant grinned as he thought about how wonderful it would be to make love in the outdoors, with the possibility of being seen adding to the thrill. What a gas. Could he convince his conservative little wife to do something a little outrageous?

Sandy knew exactly what was going through her husband's mind, and she didn't think she'd mind too much if they made out a little in the open air. She'd never done anything like that before, but the beer was getting to her and somehow tonight things felt different. The cool breeze, the moonlight on her husband's sexy chest . . . She was feeling a little wild. Without giving it too much more thought, she pulled off her shorts and panties. "I don't think my *parts* have ever been exposed to the outside air without any covering," she said.

"This is nice, isn't it?" Brant said as he pulled off his shorts and briefs. If it hadn't been before, it was now completely obvious to Sandy what was on her husband's mind.

"This," she said, reaching out and running her index finger up and down his erection, "is very nice." What had come over her? she wondered. She was feeling sexy and brave and sort of experimental. Was that what soft, summer nights did to a person? If it was, she liked it.

"Mmm," Brant purred. "Very nice indeed." He stretched out beside his wife, bare skin against bare skin.

Brant felt so good against her chest, Sandy thought, as the combination of his hot flesh and the cool of the night air combined to work some kind of magic. Then he kissed her, rolling slightly so his body covered hers. The kiss was deep and sensual, tongues playing, hands stroking naked flesh. Brant's mouth wandered down the side of Sandy's neck, kissing, licking and nibbling. He nipped at her earlobe, then palmed her breast. She felt her nipple contract as they played.

She was a bit surprised when Brant suddenly stopped their lovemaking and sat up. "I've got an idea," he said, standing and extending his hand to her. "Come on."

"Where are we going? I'm not dressed, you know." Neither was Brant, and his cock was quite visibly sticking straight out from his groin. "Someone will see."

"No, they won't, and anyway we aren't doing anything that they wouldn't do if they had the chance."

"Outdoors?"

"Let's be daring." Brant pulled her to her feet, then walked over to their children's swing set. "I saw this in a porno film many years ago and right now I'm eager to try it."

As he grabbed for the seat of one of the swings, Sandy squeaked, "You've got to be kidding."

"Shh," Brant hissed, "or you'll wake the neighbors." Still holding his wife's hand, he crouched to sit on the swing. "Somehow being out in the open feels really erotic." He jumped as his bare ass touched the plastic. "Yipe. Rough too."

"Serves you right," Sandy said. Giggling, she pushed him down onto the seat, then, facing him, straddled his lap and maneuvered her legs so they were on the other side of the swing. Brant's hard cock was trapped between her pubic bone and his belly. She felt Brant brace his feet on the ground and push, causing the swing to move. "Still think this is a good idea?" she said, scratching her fingernails down his back.

"Damn, baby, you're a tiger, and I think this is a great idea." He grabbed her around her waist, lifted and sat her back down so his cock slid into her wet pussy. "But I like it this way even better."

Now they were locked together, Brant's erection deeply embedded in his wife's canal. As he pushed the swing with his feet, she felt his cock move inside of her, making shafts of heat knife through her. "Oh, God," she moaned. "That's dynamite."

Somehow Brant kept the swing moving, fucking her with every sweep. When his head dipped and his mouth found her breast, Sandy felt spasms overtake her, and in a flash of pleasure, she climaxed. "Oh God, oh God, oh God," she hissed through her teeth.

She felt Brant's hips buck, and he came as well.

She collapsed against him and felt the muscles in his arms twitch as he held on to the swing chains. "Shit, baby," he whispered. "That's never happened before. It was so fast."

"And so hot," she said, giggling again. "And wonderful."

"You're one hot lady."

"And you're one hot guy. And this was one hot evening in more ways than one."

The Cleanest Person in Town

AT TWENTY-THREE, MINDY HAD BEEN SEXUALLY ACTIVE for several years, but she hadn't ever been truly satisfied. She loved making love and the pleasures it gave her, but when she read novels about characters who had mind-blowing, earth-moving orgasms, she doubted the truth of their depictions. *Nah,* she'd think. *Nice, but not possible, at least for me. I'm just not made that way.* For her, sex was great without all the fireworks. She and TJ, the guy she had been seeing for several weeks, had made wonderful love on their last date, and he was obviously sufficiently savvy that he knew she hadn't climaxed. The following Friday he called her on it.

"Mindy, when we make love I don't want to be the only one having fun."

"Oh, TJ, you're not at all. It was wonderful."

"You enjoyed it, I know that, but you didn't come."

"It was really great." And it had been wonderful, soft and yummy, and she'd gotten quite excited. In spite of the fact that she hadn't climaxed it had been satisfying and enough for her.

"Don't evade. I'm crazy about you and I want to share great lovemaking with you, but I need some help here. What can I do to make you come?"

Mindy was a bit embarrassed by his frank question, and since she had no idea how to answer, she just shrugged.

He looked puzzled. "Don't you know what pushes you over the edge?"

Again she gave an embarrassed shrug and looked away, still silent.

He gently turned her face toward him, forcing her eyes to meet his. "When you masturbate, what does it for you? What kind of touches?"

Blushing to the roots of her hair, she pulled away and started to get her clothing. "Let it alone, TJ. What we do is wonderful." No one, least of all a guy, had ever talked to her so bluntly about masturbation.

Despite her reluctance to discuss it, he didn't let her avoid the topic. "Don't tell me you don't masturbate. Someone as sexy as you?"

She took in a shuddering breath and gritted her teeth. She cared for TJ a lot, but he was pushing her a little too far.

TJ looked shocked. "You don't masturbate. That's amazing." He held her shoulders so she couldn't avoid his gaze. "You're so responsive, so hot when we make love, and I know you enjoy it. Listen, honey. I'm delighted to be the one to give you all this pleasure, but I need you to help me get you off. If you don't masturbate, you can't know what's really good for you."

"Just drop it. You sound like those oversexed women's magazines. You make it sound like m-m-masturbation is something to be proud of." She'd been almost incapable of even saying the word. Her mother had always told her it was dirty to touch yourself, and except in the shower, she'd never done it.

"Come on, Mindy, it's not something to be proud of *or* ashamed of. And, from what other women have told me, it's the only way to learn."

"Other women?" His previous girlfriends, he'd meant. "Learn?" She was angry but slowly getting worried too. She didn't want to lose TJ, but he wanted answers that she couldn't give him.

"Listen, Mindy. You're not the first woman I've been with, and those women and I sometimes talked pretty openly about sex. After all, making love is a deeply intimate thing we share and I always want to give as good as I get. So I ask, and get helpful advice from my partners." As much as Mindy wanted him to, TJ didn't let up. "You need to learn about yourself and your body. I don't know whether this might turn out to be a long-term thing between us, but I care about you. I want our times together to be the best you've ever had, but I need you to tell me or show me what you want, what you need. How can you help me when you don't even know yourself?" He kissed her long and deeply then and changed the subject, probably hoping she'd think about it.

When she was alone later she did think about it—a lot. She had even stopped on her way home from work the following day and bought a magazine with an article titled, "Masturbation: The Best Way to Learn." Later she sat in the kitchen, eating her dinner and reading, fascinated to realize that the author of the article was saying almost the same thing that TJ had said. The article made it clear that she was missing a lot by not knowing her own body. It was hers, after all, and she could touch it if she wanted to, the author said. Could she? Should she give it a try?

The writer suggested that a bubble bath accompanied by soft, sexy music, candles and a good erotic story might give her the courage to try touching herself. Maybe . . . So after dinner she filled the tub, lit several tapers and four pillar candles, put on a new-age CD and pulled out several romance novels with love scenes she'd really enjoyed. She climbed into the warm water, picked up the book and turned to a particularly hot encounter between the two main characters.

As they had when she'd first read them, the words aroused her and she felt the familiar itch in her groin. She wanted to touch herself there, experimentally, but she couldn't quite bring herself to. *It takes a little bravery,* the article had said. *Start with more innocent places that feel good when your partner touches them, like your breasts.*

Maybe the writer was right. She knew that her nipples were tight and engorged, but she really didn't quite know how to touch them. How did TJ do it? She cupped her breast and lifted it, then scooped some warm water from the tub and poured it over herself. *That feels nice,* she thought, and did it again. The author had emphasized that she should merely do what felt good, so she soaped her hand and hesitantly slid it over her skin. *Soap. Washing. Nice excuse to touch yourself,* she told herself. Making excuses? How silly. *It is my body, and anyway no one can see.*

She slid her slippery fingers over her breast, then flicked one finger over her nipple. She looked down at herself, then blew cool air over the tightening bud and enjoyed the tension building inside her. *That feels nice.* It was difficult for her to admit that to herself. For several minutes she used the warm water and soap to tease her breasts until she could feel a familiar tightening in her belly. She loved it when TJ made her feel this sexy. He touched her pubic hair and she always loved that, and more.

Stop weaseling, she told herself. *Think of it as an experiment, for TJ. No! That's just another excuse. Do it because it feels good. Come on, you can do this.* She moved her hand down her belly and tangled her fingers in her thatch of deep brown hair. *What should I do now? Do what feels good.* She let out a puff of air. *Okay, let's see.*

She slipped her index finger into the crevice beside her clit and slid it backward. She could feel the thicker texture of the wetness that her body was producing and just kept exploring. When she touched her clit, she jumped a little. She'd touched herself there while showering, but that had been different, clinical, and it wasn't usually this big. Now she was stroking for her own pleasure, and it felt really nice. She kept rubbing.

Eventually she began to feel empty. She wanted something like TJ's penis to fill her. Again she remembered the article. The author had suggested buying a dildo. Out of the question, she thought, at least for now. What else? The author had mentioned vegetables, carrots, cucumbers, like that. She couldn't. Not really. She had also read about using a candle. A slender wax candle, one without lots of perfumy stuff. Well, she had several of those right here, white tapers she'd lit for her bath. Scentless. Her gaze landed on one perched on the toilet lid in a small glass holder. Could she? She wanted to experience it, but was she too chicken? Putting the book she'd been reading on the floor, she stared at the candle, gathering her courage.

Finally she pulled the candle from its glass cup and pinched out the flame with her wet hands. She could do this. She swished the taper around in the tub until she knew it was as clean as the water. Then, feeling brave, she dipped it beneath the surface and aimed it at her opening. She used the fingers of one hand to part her inner lips and slowly inserted the blunt end of the candle into her channel. Her breath caught in her throat. It felt so good—and she was doing it all herself!

She used her fingers to rub her clit as she slid the candle/dildo in and out. She quickly realized that it wasn't the thrusting that excited her. She clamped her muscles around the taper and rubbed herself, finding the spots that felt particularly sensual. Eventually she realized that it was her clit that needed to be rubbed. She did.

She rubbed in small circles, then along its length. Her hand trembled and her breath caught in her throat. She closed her eyes and concentrated on the sensations.

Tension built in her belly, and a bubble of something she couldn't quite describe grew inside her. She reached for it, tried to catch it, and then it happened. A small series of spasms overtook her. *Holy . . .*

It took a few moments for her to catch her breath and for her heart to stop pounding. *So that's what it's all about.* She realized that this first one had been just a small climax, but it had been more than she'd ever had before, and it was amazing. Like a whole new world. She thought about the article once more. The writer had said that orgasms often started small but would grow as she learned more and more about her own body.

As she learned, she'd gladly teach TJ. *Wow!* she thought as she stood up, wrapped herself in a towel and flipped the drain release in the tub. She lifted the candle from the bottom of the tub, dried it and put it back in its holder. She giggled. Over the next weeks she'd not only learn about her body, but she'd also be the cleanest person in town.

Build-A-Broad

❧

Date: April 30, 2082
To: The Build-A-Broad Corporation, New Detroit, USA
Re: Beta Testing Your Newest Product—BE14

Dear Sirs:

My name is Mark Geraldi and I recently agreed to beta test your Build-A-Broad Model BE14, the newest in your line of Build-A-Broad sex robots. I want to inform you not only that am I dissatisfied with your product but also that you need to remove it from production immediately, at least until major modifications can be made.

To support my admittedly dire conclusion about your latest model, I will tell you the entire story of my experiences. Please forgive my language as I need to tell this story my way.

First, about me. I'm thirty-one years old and I've been an independent computer technician and consultant for almost eleven

years. I work from my home as many of us do, but I like to go out
and party with my friends in the evening and on weekends. I've
had many girlfriends, but just over a year ago I purchased one of
your earlier models, the AG9, to allow me to work out the tensions
of my busy life. Aggie, as I called her, was wonderful. She was so
much more than the inflatable sex toys I've owned in the past, willing and able to follow simple commands. I trained her to some of
my desires, and when I didn't have a date with a real human
woman, I always had Aggie to turn to.

I was out with friends several months ago, when John asked,
"Hey, Mark, don't you own one of those Build-A-Broad robot sex
toys?"

I'm not embarrassed about it, so I said that I did.

"Did you see the ad from the company on the Internet? They're
looking for beta testers for their newest line of robots. They're
supposedly more lifelike, more—well, let's say amenable. Since
they are in the testing phase, the company will send you one for
nothing, just as long as you agree to answer questions, fill out sur-
veys and e-mail them reports detailing your feelings about the
product once a month."

"Really? That sounds like something right up my alley." I was
delighted. I'd had such success with Aggie that I was enthused.
And let me tell you right now, I had one area of prurient interest
that Aggie couldn't adequately satisfy.

The following morning I went to your website, contacted your
technical folks and sent them my resume. It took only three weeks
before your model BE14 arrived at my door. I immediately lent
Aggie to one of my buddies.

The new robot—Betty, as I called her—was gorgeous, built, in
part, to my specifications. She was blond, with shoulder-length,
soft, genuine hair, blue eyes (I've always liked blue eyes) and a

wide, sensuous mouth. She was five foot three, with a narrow waist and long legs. When she arrived she was dressed in a sexy red gown and high-heeled gold sandals, just as I had requested.

The part of her I liked best was her tits. She had tremendous 36DDs. I've always been a tit man, and Aggie didn't have breasts big enough or flexible enough for my desires. Betty seemed perfect. Your factory did a fabulous job in meeting my specifications. That wasn't the problem.

I printed out, then read, the manual that came with Betty cover to cover and even e-mailed your tech people with several questions. They have a record of a few of my suggestions to improve the instructional CD, so if you decide to modify this model and eventually release her, you can upgrade it. A few red-lined warnings need to be added too. Very important!!! You'll see why later in this e-mail.

Anyway, I followed the instructions carefully, training Betty to perform the few nonsexual tasks the printed pages said she could do. You will be happy to know that I easily taught her to scramble an egg, hook up the central vacuuming system and activate the clothes wash/dry machine. As you stated in your manual, I waited until we had developed a rapport before beginning the sexual phase of her training.

I bought her a few outfits, including your MF1465-36DD teddy, one in red and one in black. Just because I couldn't train her yet I saw no reason not to have her dressed in a sensual way. Of course, I left her home when I went out in the evenings but told a few of my best male friends about my progress. I even showed them vids of Betty wearing her sexiest clothing with her gold sandals. I particularly liked them. I have to tell you that my buddies were hot to have a Betty model, but of course, since they weren't as qualified as I was, computerwise, they'd just have to wait until she went on the market for real. I felt like the king of the mountain.

Finally, after the suggested two-week break-in period, I thought it was time to have Betty satisfy her primary function. Since she knew my voice and had learned to talk with me, I sat her down in the living room and said, "Betty, you know what sex is?"

"Oh, yes, sir." I loved watching her sensual lips form the words as she spoke. "I've been programmed in several forms of love-making."

I knew that from the manual. Supposedly she was skilled at straight fucking and hand jobs, as well as fellatio and anal sex. She hadn't yet been introduced to the specific skill I wanted, however, so I started slowly. Over the next week she ably demonstrated her ability to bring me off with her hands, and then her other orifices. She had already been programmed to understand that the most important thing in the world for her was pleasing her master, and she became quite good at it. My orgasm sent her into spasms of delight every time.

"Oh, Mark," Betty said one evening after a particularly energetic session, "I love watching your gism spurt from your beautiful cock. You have such a beautiful dick." (Note: I'm sorry about teaching her such crude language, but it excites me to hear her talk like that, and that's the object of her existence, isn't it?)

The following evening I stayed home with Betty, ready for her ultimate test. "Betty, we've been fucking for a while now, but there's one thing I've always wanted as part of my sexual experience. You've got such wonderful tits that I want to enjoy them to the fullest."

(Another note: Your Betty model does have the most wonderful breasts, not only large but soft and squeezable with nipples that become erect when she's having sex [aroused?]. I do love sucking on them.)

"I want so much to give you everything you want, Mark," she said, her voice sweet and melodic. "What can I do to please you?"

"I want to come between your wonderful tits."

"I don't understand," she said, her lovely face slightly altered due to her obvious confusion.

"I'll show you." We began by kissing. She likes it as much as I do, by the way. Then I began to knead her tits. Wow, you guys have made them feel so real. Her nipples grew as I played with them. She's learned to enjoy it when I manipulate her boobs and nipples, so she moaned and squirmed on the bed.

I pulled off her teddy (see above) and crouched over her ribs. I pressed her gigantic breasts together and buried my face in her cleavage. As always, she was smooth and warm, with a hint of the musky perfume I'd taught her to put there. She added to my pleasure by wiggling sensuously beneath me and making sexy cooing noises.

"Betty, there's some lotion in the drawer of my bedside table. Get it, please."

"Of course," she said and took a bottle of your product LO1288 in vanilla. I poured a puddle in my palm and then rubbed it all over my hardened cock. Then I buried my dick in the valley between her breasts and had at it. I fucked her tits and showed her how to flick her tongue over the tip each time it approached her chin.

It was heavenly. I was tit fucking the most gorgeous woman with the greatest boobs ever. It took no time at all for me to come, shooting my load all over her face.

"Was that pleasurable?" she asked after she'd cleaned up.

"Oh my God, yes," I said, so spent I was almost unconscious. "It was my ultimate fantasy."

Her smile was wide and knowing. She'd learned what I liked most, and I could see her storing the knowledge away in her processors.

The next several nights we fucked, always ending with my cock between her tits. About a week later, when I wanted to fuck her pussy, she wouldn't let me. "This is what you want most," she said, bending over me and surrounding my cock with her well-lubricated flesh. "Why do it any other way?"

"Men like sex different ways at different times," I told her.

"Nonsense. Why would you want anything else if this is your ultimate fantasy?"

I tried to explain, but she wouldn't hear of our doing it any other way. We fucked that way so many times over the next weeks that I was actually fantasizing about vaginal sex.

One evening about six weeks after Betty had first arrived as I was about to go out, she locked the front door and put the key into her safety compartment. (Important note: Owners should have total access to all lockable compartments on the robot's person.)

"Why go out," she said, seeming totally rational, "when you have everything you want here?" She cupped her breasts beneath her black teddy. For once, I wasn't interested in tit fucking. After so many sessions my cock was so sore I could barely sit down.

"I like to spend time with my friends too," I said. I had actually been thinking about picking up a woman and having great oral sex with her.

"But I'm your ultimate fantasy," Betty said, sounding puzzled. "What else could you possibly want?"

"Listen, Betty. You're good in bed, but let's not get carried away. I'd like to go out now, so unlock the door."

Her voice was calm, as if explaining something to a small, not-too-bright child. "Don't be silly. Why spend your money out there? We can be happy here. We can order food to be delivered and get anything else we want online. Since you do your work here and have your pay directly deposited, we'll never want for anything."

"You've got to be kidding." I rummaged through my junk drawer for the spare key to the front door.

"If you're looking for the other key, I put it away. We won't be needing it. I love giving you your ultimate fantasy and see no reason not to spend all our evenings making love. Oh, and first thing, we'll need more lotion, and I'll need a few more outfits. These must be getting tiring for you to look at. We can go to the Build-A-Broad website and order right now."

"But what about my friends? I like to visit with the guys sometimes." And women too. "They'll wonder why I've suddenly stopped meeting them."

"Oh, I've already written a few e-mails and told them that you're through with all that." She smiled at me and actually winked. "After all, I make you completely happy."

My head was spinning. Everything I thought of to get out of my apartment she'd already considered, and my efforts were thwarted at every turn. The only thing I can do that she doesn't check up on is to write to you with my monthly report.

Now that you've read my story you can see why you have to make serious changes in your Betty model. And get me out of here!!!!

Paying for It

⚜

IN THE OUTSIDE WORLD I'M PRETTY QUIET, AND NO ONE would ever guess that I have an adventurous side that shows itself in the privacy of the bedroom. Occasionally my husband, Ron, has mentioned my slightly wild side to one of his friends, but then they tease him for weeks about what they think must be his fantasies. "Do something like that? Not Angie. Never happen." Frankly, I don't really care what others think. I love good sex, and I do lots of different things to keep Ron and me satisfied.

I don't remember how the topic came up, but one evening last week I asked him whether he'd ever been to a strip club and watched strange women take off their clothes. He admitted that he had, once, at a bachelor party for his brother. I don't mind if he looks at another woman, you understand, as long as he doesn't touch. Anyway, I asked him whether he'd enjoyed it and he admitted that he had. So I had a delicious idea.

During the week, I went to the local dollar store and bought a pack of phony money, and at the other end of the mall, I treated myself to a few goodies at Victoria's Secret. I rented a triple-X-rated video on stripping and one with lots of sexy lap dancing and watched them each several times in private. By the weekend I was as ready as I'd ever be.

We had no particular plans for Sunday evening, so I slipped into the bathroom and reached into the back of the closet for my goodies. As I put on the teddy I'd bought, I began to have second thoughts. *Maybe this isn't such a good idea,* I reasoned. I'm a bit underweight and flat chested, so I feared he'd think I looked skinny and silly. *Maybe I should reconsider.* Then I heard his familiar voice.

"Hey, Angie, what are you doing in there?" Ron called through the door.

"Nothing," I said, unhooking the front of the teddy. This was a silly idea.

"Not nothing. I'll bet you've got something sexy planned." He knows me all too well.

"Nope, nothing," I said again, hesitating.

"Well, I, for one, hope it's something," he said, a grin in his voice. "You always have the best ideas."

Ron understands that even my wild side sometimes needs a little encouragement. "Maybe," I said, re-reconsidering.

"Please?" he said in his most coaxing voice.

Done. I hooked up the teddy again. It was light blue, with little bows that tied over what breasts I have and that, when untied, would free them. The crotch was detachable. I had bought blue thigh-high stockings, so I slipped them on. I looked at myself in the mirror, bones that stick out and all. *Well, Ron likes me just the way I am,* I told myself, *and this would probably lead to a night of great sex. What the hell!*

I put on a pair of strappy silver sandals, darkened my makeup and fluffed my ear-length blond hair. In for a penny. I grabbed the pile of phony bills and walked out of the bathroom.

Ron was sitting on the edge of the bed, waiting for me. "Wow, you look fabulous," he said, his gaze roaming my body, eyes wide.

I love him so much, and the look on his face was definitely turning me on. "I thought you'd like this," I said, strutting a bit, "and you've been really good this week, so you get your allowance." I handed him some money. When he looked a bit confused, I added, "Now, would you like me to put on a little show for you?"

Understanding dawned on his face. "Oh, baby. You know I would."

He reached for me, but I backed away. "It will cost you a thousand dollars." I knew there were five thousand phony dollars in his hand, and I watched him count out my "fee." I took the cash and tucked it up into the top of my stocking. I had already put a CD into the player, so I pushed the button and the song "The Stripper" began its pounding beat.

I undulated my hips in time to the music, adding a little bump and grind occasionally. I thrust my pelvis toward him, but when he tried to touch me I shimmied away. "You paid for a show, not a touch."

"How much for a real lap dance?" he asked, almost drooling at the prospect. Although I'm his wife, he was looking at me as though I were a sexy stranger.

"Another thousand," I said, and he counted out the money. He parted his knees, and I danced between them. Then I pushed his legs together, straddled his thighs and moved my groin almost in his face.

"Oh, baby," he said, grabbing me by the waist.

"Not so fast," I said, backing away. "You still haven't paid for a touch."

I saw his white teeth as his grin widened. "How much?"

"Another thousand." I put the money on the table beside the bed and felt his arms snake around me. "If you untie these little bows," I said, showing him the light blue ribbons on the bra cups, "you'll get a nice surprise."

He likes to tease too, so he untied one very slowly and parted the sides. My small, erect nipple appeared, and he pinched me lightly, just the way I like it.

"Will it cost another thousand for the other side?" he said, flicking his tongue over my erect tip.

"I'll throw that one in for free," I said, my breath catching in my throat, my knees getting weak. He untied the second cup and played with that nipple as he had the first. Then he alternated, nipping first one, then the other. I combed my fingers through his hair, pressing his face against my chest.

"I think I'm a bit overdressed for this," Ron said, moving me away and standing so he could pull off his shirt and jeans.

I stopped his hands when he started to pull off his briefs. "Not so fast," I said, now cooled down just a bit, and ready to play a little more. I could see the tip of his cock poking out the top of his shorts, so I leaned over and licked at the precome that oozed from it. I stood then and rubbed my nipples over his chest, holding his wrists lightly so he couldn't grab at me.

I played with him for several minutes, rubbing, nipping, licking, all the while holding his hands. "Wanna touch me again?" I asked.

"You know I do," he said, panting, his voice gravelly.

"That will cost you the rest of your cash," I said.

He pushed me back onto the bed and reached for the remainder of his bills. "It's all yours," he said, holding the money above me and slowly spilling the green and white rectangles all over my body. It felt deliciously sensual as he fell on top of me, a few bills caught between us. "You know how much I want you by now," he growled.

"So take me," I said. When he started to try to unhook the many fastenings on the front of the teddy, I said, "The crotch unhooks for easy access," parroting the tag that came with the outfit.

He leaned over and quickly figured out the arrangement, then released the crotch and tossed the small piece of soaking wet, light blue fabric onto the floor among the bills. "It feels like you've been teasing me forever," Ron said. "Now it's your turn." He found my clit with his fingers and rubbed the way he knows will make me crazy. "Want my fingers inside you?"

"God," I said, barely able to get the words out. "Yes."

"Too bad," he said, "that will cost you a thousand."

"Anything," I panted, "take it all." He picked up the pile of bills from the bedside table and tucked them into the waistband of his briefs. Then he thrust two fingers deep inside of me, sawing in and out, rubbing my clit with the other hand.

"Want to get fucked?" he growled.

"I've got no money left," I said, wanting his big cock in me right then.

"No more money?" Ron said, grinning. He pulled off his briefs, money falling everywhere, and took his cock in his hand. My eyes were fastened on his fingers as he rubbed his erection, causing more fluid to leak from the head. "Maybe I want lots more cash."

Puzzled, I said, "That's all there is."

"Then you'll have to work off the rest by doing this again next week."

Isn't he wonderful? "Anything you say."

Then he was inside me, pounding, giving me what I needed. I was filled with him, and he was driving hard, faster and faster. I wrapped my stocking-covered legs around his waist and linked my spike heels together, holding him tightly against me as his hips drove his big cock into me.

"Baby!" I screamed. "Do it, hard."

"Yes, yes," he yelled, thrusting, my body in perfect sync with his. We came at almost the same moment, then collapsed, still covered with fake bills.

Later, when he could speak again, he said, "You almost didn't do it. I am so glad you changed your mind, baby."

I took a deep breath. "Me too. That debt I owe you is bothering me though," I said. "How ever will I work off so much money?"

Ron propped himself on one elbow and pulled a damp bill from my shoulder. "We'll think of a way. I promise." And I know we will.

Flying

"YOU'LL NEVER BELIEVE WHAT THOSE FOLKS ACROSS THE aisle are doing," Jean hissed quietly to her husband, Eric. Jean had the aisle seat in the first-class cabin on the red-eye flight to England she was taking with her husband to discuss a corporate buyout. She'd never flown first-class before and had enjoyed everything about it, from the liberal amounts of champagne the flight attendant had poured to the real silverware and glasses they'd used for their filet mignon dinner. They'd watched two movies, and now most of the cabin was quiet, the majority of passengers trying to get a little sleep. A half hour before, she'd settled back in her seat to do likewise, but excitement had kept her wide-awake.

She really shouldn't be so "small town." With Eric now a senior vice president of the software game company he and several of his college friends had founded two years earlier, the money was almost literally rolling in. Flying first-class was just one of the perks of Eric's having had a brilliant idea and the balls to take the chance, leaving a good job to start the company with two old college buddies. Now they were flying to London so that a much larger company could offer them many millions of dollars for their stock.

As she tried to relax she'd noticed what was going on across the aisle. "Have a look," she said to Eric, sotto voce.

Eric leaned forward and, looking across Jean's body, saw what she'd seen. The blanket over the young couple was moving rhythmically, and it was quite obvious what they were doing. "Bravo for them," Eric said with a quiet chuckle. He leaned back into his seat, a small smile still on his face.

"I'd heard about the mile-high club, but I never thought it could really happen," Jean whispered. "I guess I always pictured a couple in one of those tiny bathrooms, doing it on the toilet or something." She looked again. "It looks like she's jerking him off." She couldn't decide whether she was shocked or amused, so she opted for amused.

Eric reached over the armrest and swiped his hand over her sweater-covered breast. "Does the idea turn you on?"

Did it? She hated to admit it, but it did. She didn't consider herself a visual person, and X-rated films always left her uninvolved. However, this was real people doing real things, not actors pretending. She looked to her right again. The guy wasn't acting. She could see that his eyes were closed and his breathing jerky. Jerky. She giggled inwardly at her pun. She turned back to Eric. "Yeah, I guess it does," she whispered.

Eric pushed up the armrest so there was nothing between them, then slipped his hand beneath the hem of his wife's sweater and found the bare skin over her ribs. He used his fingernails to scratch light furrows down her side. "It turns me on too," he said, his voice low and gravelly. "Sit real still and let's see what I can do to you without anyone knowing." They had been given blankets when they'd boarded and both were covered from waist to ankles. Eric reached over and pulled the blanket up until it covered Jean's chest loosely. Then his fingers found her breasts.

As Jean was about to slap Eric's hand away, he whispered, "If you react too strongly someone will guess what we're doing. Why don't you see whether you can just ignore me?"

"You know I can't," Jean hissed.

Eric leered at her. "Good."

Jean was wearing a satin bra so her husband's fingers slid over the slick surface. She felt each movement as if it were being done with a heated brand. "That's not fair," she said, torn between laughter and embarrassment.

"Who said anything about fair?"

Jean grinned. "I did." She burrowed beneath the blanket that partially covered them both and found Eric's belt buckle. "And I've decided that fair's fair."

Eric's laugh was soft and deep. "You're right," he said, pinching her nipple.

Fortunately Jean's small squeak was lost beneath the sound of the plane's engines. She felt her breathing quicken and her pulse pound; then she squeezed Eric's erection, hard beneath the zipper of his jeans. She heard his breath catch. It was becoming a contest: who could outdo whom.

She unzipped his fly while he unfastened the waistband of her jeans. Soon each had probing fingers in the other's underwear. Jean was soon torn between the joy of giving her husband pleasure, obvious by his rapid breathing and closed eyes, and enjoying what his fingers were doing. Then he found her clit and she lost her ability to concentrate. She had his hard cock trapped between her palm and his belly and was idly rubbing the length of his shaft, but she could no longer think about what she could do to him next. Rather, she let out a long breath, rested her head against the seat back and let herself go with his ministrations.

After four years of marriage, Eric knew her reactions very well and he knew what made her crazy. He tunneled through her folds until he had one finger on either side of her clit, and then squeezed lightly. She saw colors then, swirling whirls of violet and orange, deep gold and crimson shapes blending and melding. She felt her orgasm gather deep in her belly, then bubble up. She squeezed her eyes tightly shut and concentrated on not screaming as she came.

After several moments of calming, she decided that two could play this game, so she pulled herself out of her orgasmic cocoon and wrapped her fingers around her husband's erection. Still panting from her climax, she stroked the length of Eric's stalk from base to tip, then circled his wet cock head with her nail. She heard the distinctive hitch in his breathing and felt his dick twitch in her palm. She wanted to lean over and take him in her mouth, but she couldn't figure out how to do it without everyone around them noticing. So she settled for sliding her fingertips down between his legs and, as he parted his knees, lightly scratching his sac in a way she knew would drive him crazy.

Eric pulled his hand from her clothing and, beneath the cover of the blanket, pressed her hand more tightly against him as he jerked and semen flowed from him. They sat for long moments as they both caught their breath. Luckily, she had kept several of the cloth napkins from their meal service, and she surreptitiously slipped them to her husband so he could clean himself up before making too much of a mess.

Eventually, when they were calmed and more organized, they looked back at the couple across the aisle. The guy leaned across and said, "Flying first-class makes everything so much more comfortable, doesn't it?"

They knew. Mortified, Jean held her breath, then the four burst out laughing. "Can I get you anything?" the charming flight attendant asked.

"Nope," Jean said through the hilarity. "I think we have everything we want."

Rewind Time

✦

WHAT WOULD YOU DO IF YOU COULD REWIND TIME? INTER-esting question and one Tony Perelli had to answer last winter. It all came about this way.

Late one morning Tony headed to a nearby ATM to get some cash before grabbing lunch. As he watched, a slightly wizened little man clicked something in his hand, causing Tony's ears to ring. Then the man turned, stared at his hand, puzzled, and, leading with his shoulder and without looking up, ran straight into him. Although the man was only a fraction of Tony's size, his momen-tum knocked Tony to the ground while the man remained on his feet. "Hey, what the . . ."

"I'm so sorry," the man said, shoving what looked like a pocket watch into his coat. "So sorry. I got a little disoriented for a mo-ment."

Tony's forehead hurt like hell and when he touched it, his fin-gers came back bloody. Despite the fact that it had quite obviously been an accident, the little man looked terribly upset, so Tony said,

"It's nothing. Don't worry about it. I'm fine." He picked himself up and dusted off his Windbreaker.

"Not fine at all. You might have a head injury. Please." He motioned to a bench at a bus stop. "Sit. We'll sit together until we're both sure that you're fine."

Tony was a little shaken up, and the man seemed so distraught that Tony decided it might be best to sit for a few minutes. The man handed him a handkerchief, and Tony blotted at the small bloody spot. Then the two walked to the bus-stop bench and sat down, side by side. "My name is Ainsley."

Tony held out his hand. "Nice to meet you, Mr. Ainsley, even if it was under these circumstances. I'm Tony Perelli."

"Nice to meet you, Tony," the man said, shaking Tony's hand.

"So what had you so agitated after you went to the ATM? You almost dropped your watch."

"My watch? No, no. It's not a watch. Not like any watch you've ever seen anyway." Mr. Ainsley looked deeply sad and dejected. "And it's useless."

"I'm so sorry," Tony said. "Maybe it can be fixed."

"I assure you that it's not the kind of problem that can be fixed." The man reached a trembling hand into his pocket and pulled out the oversized watch. "It's not broken; it's just useless."

He put the watch into Tony's hand. The face looked like an ordinary, if slightly ornate watch, but there were buttons all around the bezel. "This is quite something," Tony said, impressed with the complicated instrument. "Wow. This must be a timer, stopwatch, lap counter and everything. It's got all the doodads I've only seen on really expensive ones."

"I'll say it's a stopwatch of sorts, but it's useless." When Tony looked puzzled, the man continued. "I got it from someone—well, there's no need to tell you that part. Anyway, it's not just any old watch. This one rewinds time."

"I beg your pardon?"

"You push this button," he said, indicating one of the many around the face of the watch, "and that marks the start. Then, when you're ready to rewind time, you push this other one, and it rewinds to your marker. No one involved remembers anything about the period you've rewound. The problem is that you can't take anything back with you." He wrinkled his nose. "I thought I could take money from the cash machine and then have my balance restored, but it doesn't work like that." He held out his empty hand. "See? No money. It's useless."

"You mean it works kind of like the movie *Groundhog Day*?"

"Yes, yes, yes. Like that, but not a whole day, just shorter periods of time. And using it, you have the same problems that guy had."

This guy's some kind of nut, Tony thought. *He can't really believe this nonsense. There's no such thing as being able to rewind time.* Sensing Tony's skepticism, the man said, "I'll show you." He gazed at the watch, then pushed one button. "Study the people walking by and don't move. I'm holding your hand so we're connected and you'll remember, sort of." He waited a minute, then pushed another button. Flash. The people were back where they had been when Ainsley pushed the marker button. "See?"

He did see. *Holy shit. The silly thing works. Rewind time,* Tony thought. *I could do anything I like, then just rewind time.* What a gas. Ideas whirled through his mind. Races, stocks, roulette in Atlantic City. *This guy's got no imagination.*

"I've been playing with it for several days and it won't do anything useful." Shaking his head rapidly, Ainsley slapped the watch into Tony's hand. "Here, you take it." He showed him the various buttons. "You figure something good to do with it. I give up." The man stood and started to walk away. "Oh, there is one more thing."

Ahh, here's the catch, Tony thought.

"You can't rewind more than twenty-four hours," he said over his shoulder. "If you go over a day the marker unsets itself. That's it."

As the little man pulled his jacket around him and hustled away, Tony held the watch in his hand. He had plenty of ideas. *You can't take anything back with you,* the old man had said. *But,* thought Tony, *you'd have your memories.* He could look at the tote board at the local Off-Track Betting place, then go back in time and bet on the right horse. He tried it at the OTB on the next block before he went back to work but found that he couldn't quite focus his mind on the winning numbers.

He pushed the button to set the rewind just before the stock market closed. That evening he bought a paper and looked at the closing prices of a few stocks, but when he rewound time he couldn't quite remember what he'd seen. He thought about making notes, but then he realized that he couldn't write anything down because he couldn't carry anything back with him. Maybe Ainsley was right. Maybe it was useless. The powers that be wouldn't let him benefit financially. He wasn't ready to give up on the watch, however, so he spent that evening mulling over the situation.

As he considered his alternatives, he realized there was one area of his life in which he could certainly use the ability to rewind time. Women. That was it. He could pick up a girl, make mad, passionate love to her and if anything went wrong, as it usually did, he could rewind time. That way he'd have the memory but there would be no consequences. He could be a stud with Angela in the office. He'd been watching her since she joined the accounting firm he worked for, trying to get up the nerve to ask her out.

Slipping the watch into the pocket of his Windbreaker the following morning, he hurried to work. All day he watched Angela, his eyes following her sexy walk every time she got up from her desk. Finally, as quitting time approached, he clicked the marker button on the watch. Then he stood and strode around the partition into Angela's cubicle. Nothing ventured . . .

"Hi, Angela. I was wondering whether you might like to have a beer with me. If you're not busy, that is."

Angela looked up, startled. She was so lovely, with large brown eyes and long, straight, deep brown hair, caught back with a gold barrette. She had full lips and cute little freckles over her nose. "This is sort of sudden, but, well, thanks, Tony," she said. "I'd love to."

Amazing. He hadn't really expected her to agree. "Wonderful. See you at the elevator in five minutes."

Fifteen minutes later they sat at a high-top table at the little place on the corner, talking. He was suave, a little daring, and charming. He had no fear of making an ass of himself because he could always rewind time. As the evening progressed he asked about her boyfriends, and she said she had no one at the moment. He told a few jokes and she laughed, actually seemed to enjoy them, then told a few of her own. They laughed a lot.

They ordered nachos and a plate of mozzarella sticks and continued to talk. He was at his best, even better than his best. Finally, after a small pizza at a place nearby, he realized that he had nothing to lose, so he asked, "How about some coffee at my apartment?"

She hesitated and he reached into his pocket to push the rewind button, but then she said, "Sure. I'd like that."

His apartment was within walking distance, so they put on their coats and set out. During the trip, Tony turned the conversation into more erotic areas. He took her arm and tucked it under his so he could rub the side of her breast through her jacket. She didn't push him away.

In his apartment, he made coffee and they settled on the sofa. He stroked her hair. "I think you're really sexy," he said.

"No, I'm not," she responded in a soft voice, "but I'm glad you think so."

She closed her eyes and lifted her chin. *She wants me to kiss her,* Tony thought, totally surprised. This was where things usually fell apart for him. He leaned forward and gave her his best kiss. She pulled back, smiled, then cupped the back of his head in her palm and kissed him back.

Her mouth was soft, gentle, almost caressing his. She made a little humming sound and he felt the buzz on his lips. She tunneled her fingers through the back of his hair and opened her mouth. He plunged his tongue inside, but she pulled back and softly stroked his tongue with hers.

They kissed for a long time; then she lifted his hand and put it on her breast. *Shit!* He was in heaven, and his cock knew it. He was instantly hard and throbbing. He kneaded her breast, and her hand showed him how she liked it. A few moments later, he slid his palm down her belly, knowing that he could do anything, then rewind time.

She let him slip his fingers beneath the waistband of her slacks, then unbutton them. *Be bold,* he told himself. *You've got nothing to lose and everything to gain.* He could do the things he had always wanted, so he found the elastic of her panties and delved beneath. He felt her pussy hair, so hot, and then her slit, so wet. He played, exploring, probing, and with each adventure, she slid farther down on the couch until she was stretched out beneath him.

He rubbed his hard-on against her mound, then unzipped. He didn't need too much technique. He could rewind time. Soon they were naked and his hands were on her bare skin. His mouth found one erect nipple and he sucked, but not for long. He didn't want to wait, and he didn't have to.

Somehow, even though he was pretty sure he could rewind time, it was always possible the watch wouldn't work. He didn't want consequences of any kind, so he found a condom in his wallet and unrolled it over his stiff cock. Miracle of miracle, she readily opened her legs for him. He slid inside of her, propping himself on his palms and looking down at the expression of pure bliss on her face. He watched her closed eyes and felt her hands rake his back to pull him closer.

He thrust, loving the slapping sounds of their bodies as they fucked. She held him tightly, then she came! He felt it with every fiber of his being. Her body jerked and her vaginal muscles clenched around his dick. God, it was amazing, and he let himself come as well.

He collapsed on top of her and they just lay together silently for a long time. Then he eased himself out of her, and as he cleaned up, she just watched him.

Okay, here it comes, he thought. *Now the repercussions, the name-calling. Okay, I'm a bastard and I'll hear it, chapter and verse.* He glanced at his jacket lying on a chair and thought of the watch in the pocket.

"That was wonderful," Angela said softly. "You were both able to read what I wanted and able to take control when I wanted you to. I've never known anyone like you."

Holy shit! "I'm glad you were satisfied," he said. "That's what I wanted."

"Oh, I am. Very much so." She sat up and he handed her her clothing. She was grinning from ear to ear. "You know, Tony, I've been hoping for a long time that you'd ask me out. I didn't have the nerve to ask you."

"That's great. Can I see you again?" he asked as she dressed. "Maybe Friday night?"

"I'd love to see you again, but do we have to wait until Friday? It's taken so long for us to have this first date. Could we maybe have dinner tomorrow?"

I don't believe this, he thought. "That would be wonderful." He kissed her again and she eagerly returned his kiss. She peeled off her clothes and they made love again.

Later, after he put her in a taxi to send her home, he sat on the edge of his bed, watch in hand. He shook his head. *Rewind time? Not on your life.* He put the watch carefully on his bedside table. He couldn't wait until the twenty-four-hour period was over and the watch reset the rewind mechanism. He wanted no risk of time rewinding. No, sir. He wasn't letting go of this evening for anything. Maybe he'd use the watch some other time for some other purpose, but for now he had everything he wanted.

Watch

⁂

IT HAD BEEN QUITE A PARTY, A WEDDING SHINDIG FOR THE son and now daughter-in-law of close friends, and Easton and his wife, Gwen, had enjoyed every minute of it. It had been held at a downtown New York club and the couple had left only when the hired combo had stopped playing and packed up their instruments. They'd talked with Anna and Mark and all the friends and relatives and wished the newlyweds a fabulous honeymoon. "I mean, what could be bad about a honeymoon?" Gwen had said at one point.

They had both consumed a bit too much alcohol, but since they lived in the heart of New York City, they never had to worry about drinking and driving. Cabs were prevalent; they'd easily flagged one down, climbed in and given the address of their upscale, East Side apartment building.

Both were feeling horny, so on the ride uptown in the taxi, they kissed and made out like teenagers, giggling softly at the looks they received from the driver when Easton reached down the front of his wife's low-cut dress and played with her engorged nipples.

She'd sighed with contentment, arched her back and helped him maneuver one breast from the dress. She glanced into the rearview mirror and caught the cabbie's eye, amused, but slightly worried about getting into an accident.

For long minutes as they drove up Park Avenue, Easton had suckled, making loud slurping noises. Then they'd kissed deeply, putting all the passion they felt into the hot meeting of their lips. As they devoured each other, Easton continued to play with his wife's breasts while she grabbed his erect cock through the front of his dress slacks and fondled him.

She slowly unzipped his fly and pulled his hard yet velvety-smooth cock through the opening. As she began to stroke it from base to tip, Easton slid his hand up her stockinged thighs, found her waiting pussy and rubbed the length of her slit. Her entire body quivered with the need for his erection inside her.

"I want you," she moaned, trying to drag herself back into reality, if only for the few remaining minutes it would take to get home. She glanced again into the taxi's rearview mirror and saw the driver's eyes flick back to the road. It made her even hotter to know that he'd been watching.

"I've noticed how wonderfully ready you are," Easton said, his breathing noisy.

The cab pulled to a stop, but neither noticed, again deep into passionate kisses. "Sorry to break up your evening," the driver said, sounding reluctant, "but we've arrived and your doorman is rushing out to open the door for you."

Gwen raised her head and saw that they were indeed in front of their luxurious building entrance. The concierge had hustled out and was opening the taxi door just as she straightened her bodice and pulled her skirt back down. Easton zipped up, then rapidly paid the driver, adding a large tip.

It would take almost five more minutes until they reached their forty-fourth-floor apartment, and Gwen wasn't sure she could wait, but of course, she'd have to. She watched her husband talk quietly with the concierge, who returned to his desk in the large, marble lobby, with a nod to Easton and a wide grin on his face. The couple entered the leftmost of the four elevators, and Easton pushed the button for their floor.

"Have you ever noticed that the walls of these cars are mirrored?"

Gwen smiled, trying to tamp down her desire. "I often put makeup on in here when I'm running behind schedule," she said, trying to concentrate on her husband's words. The walls and even the ceiling were mirrored, the glass kept gleaming by a staff of janitors. Only the floor was not glass. Rather, it was thickly carpeted.

"Mirrors have always been a favorite pastime of mine," Easton said as he pulled at a switch on the elevator control panel and the car stopped. Gwen looked at the lights and saw that they were between the twentieth and twenty-first floors. "Have you ever watched yourself be kissed?"

"What the heck are you doing?" Gwen asked, staring at the engaged emergency stop button. "The alarm will go off."

"No, it won't, and I mentioned to the guy in the lobby that I might need to stop the car for a few minutes. He took one look at you and got the message. He won't bother us unless we call him." She looked at herself in the mirrored wall, tousled and flushed, her lips puffy from kissing. Her hair was a mess, no longer pinned up but rather falling loosely around her shoulders.

"You didn't." She couldn't help but laugh although she was also scandalized. Would she ever be able to look that doorman in the eye again? "You've got to be kidding," she said, amazed at her husband's audacity. At any other time she wouldn't have dreamed of doing anything like this, but she'd had quite a bit to drink and was feeling adventurous and daring.

"Not in the least. He'll be discreet—I tipped him well to make doubly sure. Come here." He quickly pulled his wife's coat off and dropped it on the bench at the back of the elevator. Then he pulled the shoulder straps of her dress down until her upper body was exposed. Since she wore no bra, her breasts were bare, her nipples showing her obvious excitement, her skin slightly reddened from the abrasion of her husband's heavy five o'clock shadow. Then Easton turned her around until her back was against his chest and cupped her breasts in his cool hands. "Watch," he purred, and met her eyes in the mirrored wall of the elevator. It was erotic, more so since she was bare to the waist and he was still wearing his tuxedo.

Her gaze dropped to her chest as he tugged at her nipples. "See how my fingers play with your soft, white tits?"

She stared, the sight of his dark hands on her pale skin doubling her pleasure. She both saw and felt the tips of his fingers press and pull at her breasts, the most sensitive part of her body. His mouth dropped to that tender spot where her neck met her shoulder, and as he played with her flesh, he licked, then bit her there.

When she allowed her eyes to close, she heard her husband's voice. "Don't close your eyes. Watch." She opened her eyes. It was like watching a triple-X-rated film.

His adept fingers slipped lower and snaked between her belly and her dress. "Look at my fingers," he said as he pulled her dress down until it pooled at her feet. Her panties quickly followed. As the fingers of one hand played with her nipple, Easton combed the fingers of the other through her thick, dark pubic hair. "Watch." He bit her neck. "And watch your face as you take your pleasure."

She looked at herself, fallen hair, breasts bearing the imprints of his fingers, heaving as she tried to breathe. She looked like a wanton hussy, which was probably what she was, but she didn't care.

Then Easton's thumb found her swollen clit and caressed it, eventually sliding his fingers more deeply into her slit, finding her opening, sopping wet and slippery. She parted her knees, barely able to stand as he pushed her closer to orgasm. "Watch," he whispered, his breath hot in her ear, "as you come."

She did come hard, eyes open, seeing her face flush, her pupils dilate and her mouth open wider to try to get air into her lungs. Her knees were spread, encouraging his hand to do its magic. She swallowed her moan and held on to his arm to keep from falling.

They stood like that for several minutes as she calmed. Then she dropped to her knees. "Now you watch," she purred, unzipping him and pulling his cock from his pants. "Watch as I suck your cock."

She flicked her tongue over his erection, then slowly, very slowly, took the length of him into her warm, wet mouth. She glanced at their reflection and saw her face buried in her husband's crotch, head bobbing in the age-old rhythm. She tasted the saltiness of his precome and smelled the scent of his arousal. It all combined to inflame her senses.

She wrapped one hand around him as she sucked, then used the other to rub her again-erect clit. She rhythmically stroked his cock and rubbed her slit until they both came. She was barely able to swallow his semen as waves of climax rolled over her.

Long minutes later, carrying her clothing and wrapped only in her coat, she and her well-satisfied husband arrived at their floor, unlocked the front door and stumbled into their living room. Gwen looked at Easton and started to laugh. "I don't believe we did that," she said between bouts of laughter.

"I believe it," he said, his deep chuckles joining hers. "Remind me to tip George again in the morning."

"I'll also remind you to have the walls and ceiling of the bedroom mirrored."

The Cowboy

❧

I'VE ALWAYS HAD A THING FOR COWBOYS: TALL, SEXY, good-looking, tight jeans– and boots-wearing, drawling cowboys. Here's the fantasy I've had in my mind for years. I lie in bed many nights, hands on my breasts and a vibrator between my thighs, dreaming about my cowboy.

I'm a reporter sent to a ranch in east Texas to do a story about a champion rodeo rider. What I know about rodeos could be written on a grain of rice with a ballpoint pen, but my editor picked me, and I don't refuse my editor. Anyway, the chance to meet a real cowboy, up close and personal, is too good to pass up.

I've no idea exactly where my fantasy takes place. All I know is that I drive to his ranch through hill country, with gorgeous vistas, mountains, cacti and other Texas stuff. Actually, I've created this fantasy out of whole cloth since I've never been to Texas at all, but who really cares about the scenery except that it sets the mood?

Anyway, his house is much more than the rambling wooden structure in those old Western movies. It's modern, almost starkly so, with lots of glass and stone. As I drive up, a handsomely tall, blond, curly haired, blue-eyed stud opens the front door and waits to usher me inside. He's wearing just what I want—tight jeans that outline his "package," a wide leather belt with a silver and turquoise buckle and a plaid shirt with a little string tie. His beautifully tooled boots add several inches to his already more than six-foot height. His face is deeply tanned with pale smile lines around his eyes. He's got a heavy mustache over thick, sensual lips.

"Well, hi there. You must be the gal from the magazine. I've been expecting you," he drawls. *Gal.* I love being called that and I melt, locking my knees to keep from dropping to the ground. He reaches out to shake my hand.

I take it. It's warm but callused, the hard, strong hand of a working cowboy. "Yes, I'm from *Western Life and Times*, and my name is Leslie Morgan. It's nice to meet you, Mr . . ."

"JJ. Everyone calls me JJ. Come on in." As he turns, I notice that the jeans cup his tight buns and that his ass muscles ripple as he walks. Unconsciously I lick my lips.

I look around as we walk through the spacious rooms. The entire house is an eclectic combination of Southwestern casual and New York modern, and although it seems it shouldn't blend, it does. In the living room I make myself comfortable on a long, nubby oatmeal sofa. JJ sits beside me, relaxed, with one ankle propped on his other knee. "Your editor called me and told me he'd be sending a Ms. Morgan. Somehow I didn't picture someone so young and lovely."

"Call me Leslie," I say, swallowing hard as the heat of his nearness envelopes me, "and thanks for the kind words." *Keep it light,* I tell myself. Just because he's the sexiest man I've ever seen, I'm not going to forget about my assignment. And anyway, he might not be as attracted to me as I am to him. After all, he's probably trained to give interviews like this and get flattering write-ups.

"It can't be the first time you've heard them," he says. "Someone as gorgeous as you must hear flattering things all the time."

I can't help blushing, just as I can't help getting turned on by his soft drawl that makes even the most ordinary words seem like caresses. He smiles, with a knowing look that says he can feel the erotic tension that is already sparking between us. It's affecting him too, I think.

Then it's evening. We've had dinner and the sensual air around us has gotten almost too thick to breathe. I want him, and he knows it. I'm pretty sure he wants me too. "There's a beautiful view of the sunset from the back of the house," he says.

We walk out through sliding-glass doors, and indeed the view is spectacular. But I'm not looking at the gold and rose lights that make the desert glow and back light the tall, stately cacti. I'm looking at him, and he's looking at me. It's like something out of a Western romance novel, but it's real to me. He takes me in his arms and brushes his lips over mine. His thick, brushy mustache tickles my upper lip, and his breath is hot on my face. "You feel it, don't you, darlin'?" he drawls.

I try to answer, but I can't take in enough air to form words. I merely nod.

"I mean to have you," he says, "but let's go at this real slow. I love anticipation and want to savor every moment. I have a great hot tub. How about a dip?"

I nod and he crosses the patio toward an aboveground spa and lifts the heavy cover. While he puts the lid aside, I watch his biceps and well-developed shoulders. He's like a bodybuilding infomercial.

"I hope you're not shy," he drawls, and I shake my head, glad I don't have to form words.

As I watch his long fingers, he unbuttons his shirt, and I almost drool as he reveals his broad chest and tight abs. His upper body is covered with a light dusting of pale hair, arrowing down to his navel. I'm transfixed as he unbuckles his leather and turquoise belt and slides his jeans down his slim hips, toeing off his boots and pulling the pant legs off. He's not wearing briefs, and as he turns away from me, I can appreciate his muscular butt and thighs. He flips a couple of switches and the patio lights dim and the light from one side of the tub comes on. Steam rises from the surface of the water as he climbs in and settles on the bench seat. God, I could watch him move forever.

In my dream, I've got a fabulous body: high, firm breasts, a flat stomach, narrow hips and long, shapely legs. I'm not ashamed to slowly remove my clothes as he now watches me. When I'm naked, I stand and let him look his fill, then climb in. The water is a perfect temperature, and I slowly settle beside him. He flips another switch and bubbles tickle my skin. Then his lips are against mine and his tongue slides over their joining until I open for him. His tongue fills my mouth, gently stroking mine. I snake my arms around his neck and comb my fingers through his curly hair, drawing his body closer.

When his chest hair touches the tips of my breasts I rub against him like a cat in heat. "God, you feel good, all woman," he purrs, "so soft and warm."

The sound of his words in my ear cause my entire body to tremble. His hands slide down my back and press at the base of my spine. We are now flesh to flesh along the entire length of our upper bodies, my hardened nipples raking his skin.

He cups one breast and lifts it to his mouth, drawing one tight nipple inside. His tongue performs magic and shafts of heat rocket through me, causing my back to arch until I'm still more tightly against him. "I can't wait," he growls. "Please, don't make me wait."

He cups my buttocks and lifts me until I'm straddling him. He's given me ample time to stop things, but I don't want to.

I think I would expire if I don't have him right then. His mouth still on my breast, I lower myself onto his thick shaft. The ecstasy of him filling me is almost too much to bear, and I feel my muscles clench his erection.

We remain linked for several moments, completely still, just feeling each other in the heated water. Then he begins to move inside me, his hands on my hips, lifting and releasing me. He reaches out and flips yet another a switch. Powerful jets of water buffet my body, moving it on his. I climb still higher, squeezing his erection still more tightly with my vaginal muscles.

I hear his long moan and feel his entire body shudder as he releases himself into me. I dig my fingers into his shoulders as orgasm sweeps me away too.

I've dreamed the same dream over and over, honed it to perfection, and it always ends right there, as I climax both in the fantasy and in reality. I am, of course, a magazine writer, and maybe, just maybe, my cowboy is out there, waiting for me to write his story—and more.

Colors

꧁꧂

*I*T'S THE WISP OF MAGIC THAT MAKES ME SO GOOD AT WHAT I do, and since so little is understood about this type of magic, I thought I'd write this to help you better deal with what's around you. Yes, I did say around *you*, and it is. Many people have this delightful thread of magic within them, but they've had it drummed out of them so vehemently from childhood that it's been buried. More's the pity.

Remember back when you were a child and had more of an open mind than you have now? Back when you thought you could see more things associated with people than you can now? Auras, or colors? Did you ever think you could actually peer into other people's minds? Those ideas weren't as odd as your parents would have had you believe. For generations the wonderful world of magic has been drummed out of children, and your parents probably did to you what they had had done to them. "There's no such thing as magic," they told you.

Therefore, over the ensuing years you forgot how to summon

it and soon learned to go about your life without the beautiful ability to . . . Hmm. There's no good word for the magic. Sense, feel, touch? It's difficult to use everyday words to explain something so ethereal. Suffice it to say that magic exists, but very few know it's there and still fewer know how to use it. I'm one of the lucky ones.

Let me clarify what this magical thread allows a person like me to do. Okay, first what I can't do. I can't discern the winner of the third race at Belmont. I can't make dice move in a certain way, nor do I know what the stock market will do. I can't help solve crimes like the woman on the TV show *Medium* can, although I'm a pretty fair lie detector. I can't heal your ills, or tell you who you were in some past life. What I can do, however, is touch a person with my mind, feel what he or she feels, wants and needs.

You can bet that this little talent serves me well in my chosen profession. I'm a courtesan. Okay, a prostitute, a professional entertainer of the most wonderful kind. How do I use my ability? I can—here's that word problem again. I'll use the word *feel* and although it's inadequate, it's the best I can find. I can feel your arousal, like a soft light that glows brighter and brighter the hotter you become during lovemaking. I can feel when something I'm doing makes the colors glow more or less brightly, so I'm capable of making the best love possible.

I'll tell you about a recent encounter, and then perhaps you'll understand.

Jarred's friends hired me for him as a gift, a birthday present for his thirtieth. Recently out of an acidic relationship, Jarred, they told me, was feeling terrible about himself and his sexual future. His ex had convinced him that he was a sexual boor, unable to satisfy her, and had told him flat out that this was why she was leaving.

I have a reputation as the best, so they had pooled their birthday present money and secretly hired me. That was why I was knocking at the front door of Jarred's small apartment at around six on the evening of his birthday. He opened the door. "Yes?" He was dressed as I was, in a shirt and jeans. He was nice looking, of average height, with wavy brown hair, deep brown eyes, lightly tanned skin and a firm chin. Not handsome, mind you, just sort of comfortable. And very, very sad.

"Hello," I said. "I'm Melissa—" I like that name so I use it from time to time. "I'm Melissa. Sean, Marcus and Tony hired me for your birthday."

His look changed from curiosity to disgust. "Shit, not one of those strip-o-grams. I'm really not in the mood." He tried to close the door in my face, but I had my sneaker placed so he couldn't shut it without literally pushing me out of the way.

"I'm not a strip-o-gram, as you so crudely put it." I pointed to the large wicker hamper I'd brought with me and said, "I'm a picnic and lots more."

"I said I'm not in the mood," he snapped, pushing at the door.

I reached out with my mind and touched his darkness. Birthdays weren't something Jarred wanted to think about, especially one with a zero on the end. I could almost hear him say out loud, "Thirty. Over the hill, a sexual loser without even a pick-up to spend my birthday with." You have to understand that I can't actually alter a person's mood, but I can feel why it's happening and often deal with it that way. Jarred's mood was dark, his colors deep greens and blues. I knew from the guys who hired me that he wasn't a mean or hurtful person, however, so I played on that.

"I'm sorry." I put a most dejected look on my face. "We all thought you'd be pleased to do something different tonight. Can't we just see what I've brought?" I sensed that mentioning my profession wouldn't go over too well right then. "Please? I'd hate to tell your friends that I couldn't even tempt you into a little picnic."

"Geez." He let out a deep sigh, and I could tell I was getting to him. He shook his head, then, accepting me, added, "Okay. Come on in. Let's see what the guys have come up with." He moved back into his apartment.

I stepped inside and let out the breath I'd been holding. Even I fail now and then, but this wasn't going to be one of those nights. I was over the first hurdle. The rest would be easier. Jarred took the basket from me and led me into his small but comfortable living room. Putting the hamper onto the coffee table, he said, "Okay. What have the guys put in here?"

I pulled a blanket from the basket and tossed it onto the floor, then pulled out two still-cold beers. I felt that he wanted to relax and participate, but he needed another nudge. I looked at the two bottles of beer in my hands. "Damn. I'm such a loser," I said, sounding totally annoyed at myself. "These are from some really exclusive microbrewery and they don't have twist-off caps. They need an opener. Do you have one—I hope?"

He sighed. "Sure." He was finally resigned to participating, and I could feel him warming slightly to the evening. His colors had become swirled with fewer deep blues and more muted, mossy greens. He looked at the label on the bottles. "Hey, this is my favorite. I wonder where the guys dug this up." He took the bottles from me and walked away.

While Jarred was in the tiny kitchen, I began to pull items from my hamper. Since I didn't want to crowd him, I set two places on opposite sides of the blanket with real china plates, fancy silverware and cloth napkins. I put out chunks of several different imported cheeses, two kinds of sausage, a bowl of freshly made guacamole from Jarred's favorite Mexican restaurant and a bowl of still-warm tortilla chips. I added a crusty loaf of bread and a few apples and was settling onto one side of the makeshift picnic blanket when he came back. I reached out and felt his mood. Good. As I had suspected when his friends told me about him, this approach was just right; his glow had now improved to soft lavender.

"No use letting this all go to waste, so sit with me and at least have a bite to eat. Unless you have other plans, that is."

With a small, sad smile, Jarred dropped down opposite me on the blanket. "No, I don't have any other plans, and it really was nice of the guys to do this for me. I couldn't bear this birthday thing, and I refused to let them take me out. This is nice, though." He opened and took a long pull on his beer, and then opened one for me. "Sorry, do you want a glass?"

I look several deep swallows. "The bottle is fine."

"Okay, I'll ask. Are you paid to be part of this little party?"

When I said, "I'm part of the package," he merely nodded and didn't ask any more. Deep purple slashed through his colors, but there was a fine thread of crimson as well. Crimson, the color of arousal.

With some food and a second beer, Jarred's glow had turned mostly soft yellow, but the thread of deep red hadn't disappeared. He grabbed the last of the chips, then, after we put the remains back into the hamper, he slouched with his back against the front of the sofa. "This was really nice, and I'm glad you were the one who shared it with me."

I felt he was ready to move the party along. "Actually, I'm more than just the delivery person. I'm the entertainment too."

Crimson knifed through his aura. "I don't want to misunderstand, so tell me exactly what that means."

I unfastened the top buttons of my shirt. "I think you understand quite well." As the sides of my top parted, I watched his background color leap from soft yellow to bright orange. "At least I hope you do." During dinner we'd made small talk, and I found that I had grown to like him a lot. I was also enraged at the woman who'd been so shitty to him.

I hoped he'd take it all the right way, but instead he snapped, "I get it. You're a part of this. They paid you to be nice to me, maybe even to fuck me. Make up for Connie." His words were hard and he was obviously furious. His aura was smoky and black. "Didn't they think I could get a girl of my own?" Sadly the reds were almost gone.

I touched his aura and let it guide my words. "Yes, I'm being paid, but it wasn't because they felt any lack of confidence in you. They told me that they remember what a stud you always were. They were afraid that Connie had knocked everything out of you, everything that made you what you used to be. They wanted me to help you get it back." I pulled my shirt off, and as I was wearing nothing beneath, my breasts claimed Jarred's attention. Again, bolts of bright red sparked through his consciousness.

"This is enough," he snapped, denying what I knew to be true. He wanted me. "When I want a woman, I'll find one of my own."

I picked up his hand and placed his palm on my nipple. "Why should you go looking when I'm here now?"

Colors where swirling now as we were both becoming aroused. I could feel his blood throbbing through his veins and knew the excitement of his stiffening cock. I could also see small shafts of icy blue doubt knife through him. He tried to pull away, but I wouldn't let go of his wrist. I caught his gaze and held it. "I'm worth the risk," I said, and not letting him wonder about my remark, I leaned forward and pressed my lips to his.

I tasted his colors, warm deep reds and umbers, melting into golds like the shades of a sunrise. I sensed him opening and the icy shafts fading. He parted his lips and the kiss deepened. I touched my tongue to his; then he slid his over mine. I could feel him relaxing, becoming the sensual man he truly was. I released his wrist, and, as I knew he would, he curled his fingers and filled his hand with my breast.

God, he felt good. One of the benefits of finding the thread and seeing the colors is that I make it good for myself as well. I slid down until I was lying beside him on the blanket. As he kneaded my flesh with both of his hands, I unbuttoned his shirt and slid my fingers through the mat of hair that covered his chest.

As he finally let go of the last of his reluctance, his colors nearly overwhelmed me with their brilliance. Now hot reds swirled with deep orange as his hands roamed my chest and back, his lips constantly changing position against my mouth. Then his mouth replaced his hands on my nipples, and he drew first one, then the other between his lips. My own colors matched his, and the thread between us grew stronger, tighter, pulling him against me.

"Too many clothes," he growled, and quickly we were naked, smooth flesh pressing against smooth flesh. He found a condom in his pocket and put it on the blanket beside us. I stroked his calf with the sole of my foot and felt his breath catch. Now I didn't need any special abilities to know he was fully aroused and liked what I was doing. I grabbed at his rear cheeks and squeezed two handfuls of ass. "I'm not sure I can wait too long," he groaned.

"Why wait?" I moaned, fully excited and eager to feel him inside of me.

"Are you sure?"

I marveled. Even though he knew I was bought and paid for, he was being a considerate lover, wanting my pleasure as well as his. I understood how much his body needed me right then, and I wanted him as well. "I want to feel you fill me. I need you to fill me. Please!"

He covered his cock with the condom and thrust into me. With driving strokes he pounded, coming with a roar. Still panting, he reached between us and touched my clit. "Yes," I purred. "Right there. Touch it. Stroke me."

It took only a minute or so for my legs to curl around his and my fingers to clutch at his back. My scream split the evening as orgasm overtook me, colors whirling, eddies in all the varied hues of climax whirling around the two of us. "Feel it," I said as my spasms squeezed his only partially erect cock.

"God, you're coming. I can feel you coming," he said, amazed.

Quickly he was hard again and we made love for a second time, this time more slowly. Again I came, letting him share in the spasms of my orgasm, just before he bellowed and came one last time.

"My God," he said a little while later, "it's never been like that."

"You mean it wasn't like that with Connie," I said, replete. "Maybe she wasn't the best lover in the world, or maybe you just weren't a good couple in bed. It takes two, you know."

He sighed. "Maybe you're right."

"No maybe about it," I said, and sensed that a small glow of understanding was enhancing his aura. That glow would grow, and soon he'd be back to his old self.

So that's pretty much where my story ends. However, maybe you've been with someone who seemed so tuned in to you that every move seemed perfect. Maybe he or she had, or has, that thread. Maybe that lover could see the colors. Maybe you can too, or could if only you'd let yourself go and really open to your partner. Want to try? Next time you're making love, try to touch your partner's desires, sense when he or she is moving closer or further away, when colors flare or fade. Can you do that? You'll never know until you try.

Different Colors

❧

I'M NOT AN ALIEN. NO, I LIKE TO THINK OF MYSELF AS THE next generation of being, one who can sense that aura, the colors of people's—okay, maybe the word is *soul*, but that's not what you'd call it in my line of work. I'm a courtesan, a prostitute, and the ability to feel, or see, someone's desires is invaluable. Can others do what I do? Sure, there is a whole group of us, both male and female, and we all use our talents for the betterment of mankind— personkind. Sexually.

Should we tell someone, let them try to ascertain whether we have an additional chromosome, or one too few? Let them test us, dissect us and be shocked to find out that we're just like everyone else? Not a chance, and I don't think they'd want to know. Actually I think most humans are born with this talent, but the majority of people don't use it after they reach puberty, so it just atrophies. I certainly use it. Often. And it serves me well.

At eight o'clock, Jack, a new client, arrived at my hotel suite, the one I use for "entertaining." He was about five foot ten, with a completely shaved head, large puppylike brown eyes and a well-trimmed mustache and goatee. He wasn't handsome, but when he smiled and his eyes shone, he was charming looking. Of course, he didn't have to be anything. I was bought and paid for. Well paid for.

"Hi," he said when I opened the door, "I'm Jack. We spoke on the phone a few days ago." He sounded nervous, as many of my new clients do.

"Nice to meet you, Jack," I said, taking his hand and ushering him into the living room of the suite. "I'm Melissa."

"Is that your real name?"

I chuckled. "It's as real as it gets." I reached out with my mind and touched his aura. It was totally confusing and very difficult to put into words. There were swirls of hot gold and vermillion, the hues of impending sex, but they were mixed with stripes of icy blue. He was totally impossible to read, and I was puzzled, a new sensation for me.

I extended my hand and he shook it. The contact further confused things, adding soft, shy mauve to the mix. Oh, well, I'm the best at this, and I'd eventually solve this man and give him the best evening he'd ever had. "Can I pour you a drink?" I pointed to the room's fully equipped wet bar, and he chose to have a glass of Johnny Walker Black. I poured myself a glass of white wine. More than a little alcohol confuses my senses.

I had told him on the phone that I like to get to know my clients so I can best serve them, so we settled on the sofa and talked for a while. I surreptitiously watched his colors, no closer to finding out what would please him. With his second drink the icy blue faded. *Maybe he's just nervous,* I thought. But the heat of arousal and the touch of shyness remained. What did he want? Shyness? Maybe . . .

"Would you like another drink?" I asked, taking his hand and holding it tightly. Shafts of red infused his color. *Ahh,* I thought.

I squeezed more tightly and the shafts flashed. "I think not," I said, adding a bit of force to my tone. "I think you need something quite different." I slid my hand to his wrist and grabbed, holding him strongly enough to bring him to the edge of pain. The reds brightened, but there was a hint of green as well. I understood. It wasn't the pain but rather the power that he needed. I knew him now, and I was confident that I knew how to please him.

"What do you mean *different*?" he said, not moving his hand or arm. His voice was a bit hesitant. I wondered whether he really understood what he wanted. He would before the evening was over.

"I think you need to please me. I think you need to do whatever I ask."

He looked puzzled but didn't speak.

"Tell me that you want to please me. Do it!"

His colors exploded, and, after a slight hesitation, he dropped his chin and said, simply, "Yes." His colors flared again, the red stronger but surrounded by deep greens and blues.

"Good. Stand up and let me look at you." He stood slowly. "Mmm, nice," I said. "You should do quite well." I turned, stretched my legs out on the sofa and leaned my head back against the arm. I had worn a nonspecific outfit, a short black skirt, sheer black hose and black pumps with three-inch spike heels. My satin blouse was the color of red wine, and I unbuttoned it now so lots of cleavage was visible. Golds and oranges swirled around him.

"Undress." My voice wasn't loud. It didn't need to be. Instead I kept it low but forceful.

His hands shook. I didn't need a crystal ball or his colors to know I'd hit a very vulnerable but delicious spot. "Now!" Stronger voice, stronger colors.

His fingers went to his shirt and he unfastened the buttons. Soon the shirt was thrown on a chair, followed by his undershirt. "Shoes and socks next," I said, and when those were gone he looked at me for his next instructions. God, I love finding out something so sexy about a guy. I love it even more when he not only discovers his real self but also realizes that this encounter will be the best he's ever had. "Slacks and shorts. Now!"

He still hadn't said a word. When he took a breath to say something, I merely glared at him, and he silently let the air out in a long sigh. He'd accepted our roles, I the power, he the slave. He unbuckled his belt, unzipped his slacks and dropped them. As he stepped out of them, I could see the enormous bulge in his shorts. He was fully aroused.

"I've changed my mind," I said as he tossed his slacks on the chair. "Leave the briefs on. Stand up so I can look at you." He straightened, and as I looked him up and down, his gaze lowered but his erection grew. "You're being a very good boy," I said and watched his aura suffuse with flashes of tangerine and bright apricot. "Answer 'Yes, ma'am' when I speak to you."

A shaft of blue penetrated, then dissipated. He'd had a quick doubt, but it was no more. "Yes, ma'am. Thank you."

"Good," I purred. "Now take your palm and rub it over your cock through your pants."

Again doubt filled him, then faded. He took his right hand and used the palm to stroke his erection through his cotton shorts. He would have his first orgasm that way so he'd be able to last longer the second time. I had lots that we could play with. "Rub it so it feels good. I want you to come for me, and I know you're more than ready."

"I don't . . . I never . . . I can't . . ."

"Of course you can, and you can do it while I watch your hand. Stroke! And watch my eyes stare at your hand as you do it."

He began, and when I knew he was close, I said, "Use your left hand." It would feel strange, but that would add to his pleasure. He switched hands, and it only took another moment until his entire body shook and a large wet stain covered the front of his briefs. "That was lovely," I said. "Go into the bathroom and clean up. And leave your shorts in there."

He was gone for only a few moments, but in that time I hiked my skirt up and twisted my long hair into a tight bun at the back of my neck, fastened with a clip I had in my purse. Now I looked more like a dominant woman. I sat back down on the couch.

When he returned, he was naked and his cock was semierect. "Now it's my turn," I said, leaving one foot on the carpet and stretching the other out on the couch. I snapped my fingers and pointed to a spot beside the sofa. Without hesitation he knelt beside me. "You may touch me," I said, his glow warm rose and orange.

His hands were warm and soft on the skin above my hose and his fingers skillful as he lightly brushed the fabric that covered my pubic hair. "How do you like it, ma'am?" he whispered.

Right response. "You're such a good boy," I said. "I like it with your fingers and your mouth."

He pushed my skirt up and brushed his fingertips over my crotch, making me shiver. I heard two soft purrs, his and mine. His fingers swirled over my mound, just grazing my clit. "Harder," I said, and he found my button and rubbed through my panties. "Use your mouth," I snapped.

His breath was hot as he licked and bit my flesh lightly through the fabric. I cupped my breasts and pinched my nipples.

"May I?" he asked, moving the panties aside.

"Take them off for me. With your teeth."

It took a while, but he managed to get my bikinis down to my knees. I let him finish removing my underwear with his hands since I was getting impatient.

"Do it!" I snapped, pointing to my crotch.

His hands returned to my pussy. One finger rubbed my inner

lips, and another pressed against my clit. He cupped my ass cheeks and pulled me tightly against his mouth as his tongue found my opening and plunged deep inside. I came, panting. He continued stroking me while I came down. He was good at this and, God, I love good lovemaking.

"I will allow you to enter me."

Allow? You bet! I wanted him almost as much as I knew he wanted me. I pointed to a selection of condoms I had scattered on the credenza. "Put one on."

I watched his now fully erect cock as he unrolled a Black Beauty onto his shaft, then he came back and moved me until my hips were at the edge of the sofa. When I nodded my permission, he knelt between my thighs and drove into me without hesitation. His thrusts were full and sure as he held my hips and threw back his head.

I knew he'd wait until I came again, and I did with his cock filling me. I moaned and managed to say, "You may come now," and he came as well. I could feel the twitching of his cock as he groaned.

Later he sat on the carpet. "How did you know, when I didn't?"

I smiled. "I'm pretty good at reading people."

"You certainly are, and I'd like to see you again."

Later he rose, put his clothes back on and left seven one-hundred dollar bills on the credenza. "I'll call you."

I knew he would.

A Nooner

"Eve, you shouldn't be here. I've got to work." Chris looked up from behind his large oak desk and frowned. The desktop was covered with folders and loose papers; his phone and computer sat on a credenza beside him.

"Oh, come on, baby," Eve said. "You know what they say about all work and no play." She looked him over; his serious expression matched his pin-striped suit and crisp white shirt. His tie was striped, as were all his ties. She watched Chris's sigh echo through his body as she stood facing his desk. She'd succeeded in surprising him in his new office, and now she wanted to play. Now that he had an office with a door that could be closed, she knew that she could.

She'd dressed for this, in a tight teal blue teddy with white lace over the breasts and a white satin ribbon up the front. She had bought matching stockings that she had hooked to the long garters that hung from the bottom. She'd slipped on silver sandals and pulled a raincoat on over it all. She stuck her lower lip out in what she knew looked like a deliciously sexy pout. "I came all the way here, baby, just for you."

"I have to work," Chris said, both exasperated and interested. She could see him mentally arguing with himself. "I just can't. I'm really busy. I'll see you another time."

"Now." She opened her coat and stood in front of the desk in all her glory. Fortunately the office's only windows faced the river.

"Oh, baby, please. You must know how sexy you look, but I can't. Please. Later." He was almost whining.

A loud knock sounded at Chris's office door. "Hey, boss," his secretary said from outside, "there's a Mr. Lowrey here from that accounting firm. He says he's got an appointment at one."

Chris dragged his fingers through his shaggy brown hair. "That tears it," he whispered. "Damn. He's early. My boss set this meeting up and I've got to see him. And you can't be here." Louder, he called, "Tell him I'll be right with him." Again to Eve he said, "It will be very brief. I just have to be polite. He's a friend of the boss and I have to give him a chance to give his spiel. Everyone knows we're happy with the guys we've got, but I have to humor him."

Eve tried to look chagrined but didn't succeed. She knew that Chris was a rising star at the firm. After all, he'd just gotten this real office. It would take more than her, found in his office, to upset the apple cart, but she also knew he was worried. "Okay. I'll disappear. Where should I hide?"

"You can slip into the coat closet," Chris said. She looked around and spotted the door to the closet, so she slowly walked toward it, wiggling her ass as she did so. Chris walked over, nudged her inside with a kiss on her neck and closed the door behind her. Fortunately it was late spring and there were no coats to contend with.

This is pretty silly, she thought, *but sort of fun too*. She waited until the two men were settled, then opened the closet door a crack.

Chris was facing her, while the new guy had his back to her. She caught Chris's eye and winked. Then she licked her index finger and sucked it like a cock, all within Chris's sight. She was sure that it was all he could do to keep a straight face.

"I'm so glad you agreed to see me," the other guy said. "I know you have someone and that you're satisfied, but I just want to give you some ideas on what my outfit can do for you." He started to rattle off numbers.

Still in Chris's line of sight, Eve again pulled her coat off and stood wearing only the blue teddy. Slowly she rubbed her hands over her breasts, massaging them and playing with her hard nipples. It was all she could do not to laugh as the accountant rattled on for fifteen minutes while she silently slid her hands all over her body.

"As you said yourself, we do have a firm that really meets our needs." Chris glanced at Eve from of the corner of his eye. "I'm afraid you're wasting your time."

I'm not wasting my time, Eve thought, hearing the impatience in Chris's voice.

"I realize that, but it's my time to waste," the guy said. "I merely wanted to meet you and put my company's name into your brain. If anything changes I hope you'll remember it."

Eve now slipped her hand between her legs and stroked herself. She let her head fall back, some of her pleasure real, some feigned for Chris's benefit. She licked her lips and tilted her pelvis so he could see exactly what she was doing.

Chris extended his hand across the desk, and Eve noticed that his pupils were dilated. He was hot for her and she knew it. "Thanks so much, Mr. Lowrey, for coming." With the word *coming* Chris's eyes flashed toward her. "I will certainly keep you in my mind." She didn't know whether Mr. Lowrey hadn't a clue what was going on or knew something was amiss and chose to ignore it.

The man stood and handed Chris a business card. "I thank you for your time." The two men shook hands, and as Chris rose to show Mr. Lowrey out of his office, Eve silently closed the closet door.

She heard rustling sounds and the click of a door closing. Then the door to her little hideaway sprang open. "You are one hell of a cock tease," Chris said with a leer, "and you deserve anything that happens to you." He pushed her deeper into the closet and came in after her, closing the door behind him. "Now, my dear, you're going to get the fucking you so richly deserve." He unzipped and, totally ready, pulled the crotch of her teddy aside and plunged into her. It was hard, fast and delicious. Chris came quickly, and with his hands on her ass, Eve's pleasure peaked.

Breathless, they emerged from the closet into his silent office. "You are the very devil," he said.

"I sure am. I feel like Monica Lewinsky in the Oval Office." She pulled on her raincoat and cinched the belt.

Chris's laugh was warm as he looked at his watch. "It's almost two, so go home. The kids will be getting home from school within an hour. I'll be home for dinner at the usual time, and once the children are in bed you're going to get it."

"Again?" As she reached for the doorknob, she turned, grinned at him and said, "I can't wait."

My Friend Fred

Transcribed from tapes recorded in the office of Dr. Simon Taft.
Session with Tina Malone, July 21, 2032.

DR. TAFT: You don't mind if I record our sessions, do you, Ms.
Malone?

MS. MALONE: Not at all, Dr. Taft.

DR. TAFT: Good, the machine is running. Tell me about yourself.
And tell me about your invisible friend.

MS. MALONE: Okay, Doctor, you can doubt me if you must, but
at least I know you'll listen. Isn't that what you're paid to do?

I have an invisible friend. Well, he's not totally invisible, but
I think I'm the only one who can see him. As you know, I'm
thirty-four years old, not four, and I'm not nuts. But I do have
a friend who's sort of invisible. I think he's an alien from another space or time who can't quite make it into our space/time.
Whatever. When I see him in the middle of the night, he's sort
of blurry and ghostlike, like the aliens you see in old-time TV

shows. He's sort of humanlike, with legs and arms, and a head with eyes, a nose and a mouth. The rest of his body is usually draped in some kind of gauzy material, so at first I didn't know what was beneath.

DR. TAFT: Does he have a name?

MS. MALONE: He can't quite communicate with me, so I've had to name him myself. I call him Fred. Actually he can send me feelings and ideas, just not words, like some sort of telepathy. I guess that's how he communicates in his world. Although I tried to talk to him, he didn't understand me either.

DR. TAFT: You keep calling it a *he*. He's definitely male?

MS. MALONE: Oh, most assuredly. [She giggles] All male, as you'll learn when I tell you more.

DR. TAFT: You only see him at night?

MS. MALONE: Recently I've been seeing him during the day too, although not as often. I think that means that he's getting closer to being able to cross over to "our side." His body also seems more substantial, less see-through.

DR. TAFT: And still no one else can see him?

MS. MALONE: I can't understand why not. Recently he seems quite real to me.

DR. TAFT: Getting back to what you just said, what do you mean "cross over to our side"?

MS. MALONE: You know, become someone in our time and space.

DR. TAFT: Oh. I see. Okay, tell me about your first encounter with him, in your own words.

MS. MALONE: Well, it was late at night and I was just falling asleep. Suddenly there was this light in my bedroom and he was there. Just there. One second the room was empty, and the next he was standing there.

DR. TAFT: What did you do?

MS. MALONE: Why don't you let me tell this? It will be easier all around. Good. Well, at first I was really freaked. I didn't scream, like women do in the movies. I just lay there and watched him as he looked around my room. Obviously he can see our space better than I can see his.

He seemed to be sending me calming waves too, and I found myself relaxing. He walked, if I can use that word, around the bed, studying everything on my dresser and my bedside table. He opened drawers and looked inside.

DR. TAFT: Hold it. I thought he couldn't do anything in our space.

MS. MALONE: I never said that. Not at all.

DR. TAFT: I'm sorry. Go on.

MS. MALONE: After he inspected everything in my room, he held up my hairbrush and sent me a sort of quizzical message. I decided that he wanted to know what it was, so I used sign language and mimed brushing my hair. He did that with a few pieces of my jewelry, my toothbrush from the bathroom and my shower cap. I showed him how the shower worked and what clothing was for. That all took a few hours, then he faded away.

DR. TAFT: But he came back.

MS. MALONE: The following evening. He rummaged in my drawers again, and I taught him about my iPod and my portable radio. He seemed to like music. Then he found my vibrator and held it up.

What was I to do? I tried to tell him about sex, but he didn't quite get it. I made motions like holding a baby, then tried to mime a guy with a dick. Like this. [Rustling sounds as if she's demonstrating] He seemed to get it, and he parted his robes and showed me that he had similar equipment. Actually it was fully erect and quite a bit larger than the average guy's. I nodded.

Then he was again quizzical, I gathered, wondering about my anatomy. So I showed him. I pulled off the tee shirt and sweatpants I sleep in and showed him how a woman of our planet is put together.

He understood quickly, and again was quizzical, holding the vibrator in his hand. I lay on the bed and got myself in the mood. I played with my tits. That gets me every time. He stared, then put his hands on my chest. I was really surprised that I could feel his long, slender fingers on my skin. Oh, did I tell you he has eight of them on each hand? They felt rough and really kinky on my tits. He experimentally pulled at my nipples and seemed to enjoy tweaking them and squeezing them. I certainly did, I can tell you. [Long silence]

DR. TAFT: Can you continue, Ms. Malone?

MS. MALONE: [Long sigh] I can. This is really embarrassing, but you're a doctor so I guess I can tell you everything. Anyway, after he'd played with my breasts for a while he shrugged his shoulders and I got a "what next" message. He seemed fascinated by our sexual methods. He held up my vibrator again. I tried to tell him that, if you don't have a partner, you can use it for sexual stimulation. I tried to be clinical about it, but it was difficult. I was so turned on.

I took the vibrator from him, spread my legs and showed him how I use it. As I turned it on to get some relief for myself, he looked shocked and grabbed it from my hand. Then he pulled off his robe. He was built like a well-developed human, and his cock seemed even larger than before.

He crouched over me and very slowly slipped his erection into me. I felt my body stretch to accommodate him. At first it was a bit painful but really erotic too. As my body adjusted, he began to fuck me.

DR. TAFT: Did it feel like having sex with a human?

MS. MALONE: Better. He continued to play with my breasts while he thrust his enormous cock in and out. I would swear that it grew still larger inside of me, filling all my spaces totally. Then I showed him my clit, and he readily changed his fingering from my tits to my snatch. He was by far the best, most considerate lover I've ever had. And all those fingers. You look a little flushed, Doctor. Am I upsetting you?

DR. TAFT: [Several heavy sighs] Not at all, Ms. Malone. Please continue.

MS. MALONE: [Short silence] Well, I came. My climax was better than any I'd ever had with a real man.

DR. TAFT: [Clearing his throat] Was that the last you saw of him?

MS. MALONE: Oh, no. For several weeks he came to me every night. It seemed to me that each time he got a little less gauzy and more—I don't know—substantial. His constant ministrations meant that I was horny all the time, but when I tried to bring a guy home from a bar I frequent, the room got really cold and the guy felt himself pushed out of the room. He scurried away, and I haven't seen him since. So it's just been Fred and me for the last two weeks.

DR. TAFT: You know this is all a hallucination, don't you, Ms. Malone?

MS. MALONE: That's what everyone would have me believe, Doctor, but it's not. My family got together yesterday and begged me to see you to have you straighten my head out. So here I am.

DR. TAFT: I understand. Well, Ms. Malone, this is delicate for me to mention, but all your talk of sex with Fred seems to have gotten you all excited. I can tell from your body's reactions. If you'd like to masturbate to relieve your tensions, I think it would be all right.

MS. MALONE: He wouldn't like that.

DR. TAFT: Fred wouldn't like it?

MS. MALONE: No. He doesn't want anyone but him using my body. Even me. He gets very angry.

DR. TAFT: That can't be true. He's not real. He's just a masturbatory fantasy. You have to understand that if we're going to get anywhere.

MS. MALONE: No, it's not. I know it's not. [She becomes agitated] You're making me sorry I ever came here, ever told you about Fred.

DR. TAFT: Try to calm down, Ms. Malone. Let me help you to calm down. [Rustling of clothing]

MS. MALONE: Don't touch me, Doctor. This is quite unprofessional of you. Stop pawing me. [She screams] Fred! It's all right. Don't hurt him. It's all right. Dr. Taft, he's behind you. [Crashing sounds] Dr. Taft? Dr. Taft? What's happening? [Masculine screaming, then silence]

End of tape.

The district attorney stopped reading. He'd already listened to the tape several times, but now he had also read the transcript, trying to be dispassionate. He sighed, unable to believe what he'd heard and read. "And that's all the tape contained, Ms. Frazier?"

"That's it," the doctor's receptionist said. "I transcribed it word for word."

"And you found the doctor dead in his office right after the crashing stopped?"

"I got frightened and barged into the room. I found Dr. Taft on the floor and there was no one else in the room."

"I gather from the investigating officer that the windows are sealed. You're sure there was no one else in the room? You saw

Ms. Malone enter the office at four o'clock. Where do you think she had gone?"

Ms. Frazier's voice was small and sounded a little frightened. "You said that she's disappeared. I think she went with Fred to wherever his world is."

"That's ridiculous."

"You told me yourself that Dr. Taft was killed by something much bigger and stronger than anything you'd ever run into before. What else can one think?"

"What else indeed?"

Glow

My wife, Ronnie, is amazing. We've been married for almost four years and you'd expect things to become a bit, well, let's say predictable, but she's a constant creative delight in the bedroom and elsewhere.

Ronnie is tiny, just barely five feet tall and on her heaviest day weighs only one hundred pounds. I'm almost six foot two so the contrast between us is striking. The height difference makes creative sex imperative, and we've had some delicious times in almost every room of our apartment. Sometimes she plans something particularly delicious and purposely lets me know that she's got one of her wonderfully devious ideas.

We love to go to this one club called Glow in the warehouse area of town. They use black lights and lasers to light up various parts of the dance floor and the performers. Yes, I said *performers*. Sometimes they have topless dancers and, late on the occasional Saturday night, live sex acts on stage. Nothing too heavy or out of line, just entertainment of the slightly kinky kind.

For several weeks, Ronnie had been ultrasecretive, preparing one of her little surprises. I'd been deliberately looking the other way, getting hornier and hornier waiting for her to spring whatever it was. Well, last Saturday night, at Glow, she did it. I mean, really did it. Let me tell you about it.

We got there at about ten and met a few people we knew. We danced and had a few beers. At Glow they card the patrons very carefully, don't serve hard liquor and have a four-beer limit. Since things get a bit unusual some evenings, they don't want any drunken trouble with the guests or visits from the cops. Just after midnight Ronnie leaned close to my ear and whispered, "I'm going to be gone for a little while. I'll find you when the time comes, so don't worry or go looking for me." She grinned her most seductive grin, turned, then wiggled her fanny at me and disappeared into the back of the club, I assumed to the ladies' room. We all know what *assume* means. Boy, was I wrong.

"Ladies and gentlemen, please take your seats," Glow's DJ said. "This evening's last show is going to begin in about five minutes, so take your seats or find someplace to stand quietly. It's going to get very dark in here and we don't want anyone wandering, so make those quick pit stops and get ready for a fabulous performance." When the DJ finished his announcement, he put on some nondanceable elevator music. It was more like ten minutes until the place settled down, and after one or two more announcements, everyone finally found a place to sit or stand.

I felt pretty lucky to have a seat with several friends at a table right in front near the stage, but I kept wondering where Ronnie was. I thought about going to look for her, but I trusted her and she'd asked me not to search her out. As I thought more about it, I put two and two together and speculated that Ronnie might be part of the show. She'd never done anything quite that brazen before, but I wouldn't put anything past her. I shrugged mentally and decided to roll with it and see what happened. Finally, with a musical fanfare, all the lights in the club went out. Let me tell you that, when the DJ said *dark*, he wasn't kidding. There were red-lighted exit signs and that was about it.

At first the music's volume was so low that the audience wasn't aware of it. Then slowly the sound level increased until the beat was pounding in everyone's ears. All at once we all became aware of a shape on the stage, dancing. The body was so shadowy and amorphous that we couldn't tell whether it was male or female, but the sinuous movements were highly erotic. After a few minutes the dancer's hand appeared from behind his or her back covered with glowing goo.

The hand left little doubt; the luminescent fingers, slender and tapered with long red-polished nails, belonged to a woman. I could also see the dancer's abdomen, flat and smooth, with a tiny, silver belly button ring just like Ronnie's. Was it her? I took a better look at the hand and saw it. She wore the pinky ring I'd given her for her last birthday. She could have taken it off, but I knew it was her message to me. My creative wife was going to show off for a roomful of people while I watched. I was delighted. I had no doubts about her love for me, and now all these folks would envy me. They could look, but only I could touch.

The gel on her left hand was thick and gooey, and as she danced, she spread some on her right hand. Two glowing hands now faintly illuminated a body I knew so well, curvy in all the right places. I could make out a tiny bikini, but otherwise she was naked. I could also barely make out a bucket on a stool off to one side of the stage. *It probably contains the glow-in-the-dark stuff*, I thought.

As the audience hooted and clapped, Ronnie wiggled her way over to the pail and scooped out a handful of goo. Then, as she undulated, she painted patterns on her smooth, well-muscled thighs. Stars and crescents, stripes and curves appeared wherever her finger traveled. It was highly erotic, watching parts of her body appear in the near pitch darkness. I felt my cock twitch.

The audience applauded, and several guys yelled, "Paint the good parts." She bent over the edge of the stage near me and whispered, "You know who I am?"

"Of course, Ronnie."

Louder she said to me, "Wanna play?" She backed up, her hips never still, her arms extended, fingers inviting me up onto the stage.

"I'll come with you," one man yelled.

"Pick me," another shouted.

She moved her hands in an invitation, and everyone clapped and stomped and urged me onto the stage.

I quickly climbed onto the stage with her, then gladly followed her directions and untied the top of her bikini, leaving her only wearing the thong bottoms. While the audience screamed and whistled, she slowly painted one breast with the glowy stuff. While she danced and the music pounded, her other breast appeared beneath the otherworldly blue glow. She twisted her nipples and fondled the breast I was so familiar with. She thrust her pelvis forward, then turned and painted her ass with both hands, pulling her cheeks apart and spreading the stuff deep into the crack.

When she whispered, "Take your shirt off," I quickly pulled my polo over my head. She danced close and rubbed the tips of her painted breasts against my smooth chest, leaving trails of glowing gel across my pecs. Over and over she danced close and, using her erect nipples like twin paintbrushes, swirled colored stuff over my skin.

When my chest was covered, she wiped her hands on a small towel and unbuckled my pants. "Game?" she asked.

"Of course," I said. She knew me well enough to be sure that I would play with her, even with a roomful of people watching. Although I'm not a bodybuilder, my nude body isn't too bad to look at, and I was pretty sure that few people would be looking at me anyway. She quickly stripped me, tossing my clothing to the side of the stage.

The crowd applauded at the sight of my erect cock and still louder when Ronnie reached into the pail and scooped out a handful of gel. "Shall I?" she yelled to the audience.

A chorus of female *yes*es echoed back, along with a few guys' voices yelling, "Paint me, baby."

Ronnie grasped my erection in both hands and massaged it from base to tip, then from tip to base. Along with the goo, precome was oozing down my shaft. God, I was so randy I could barely function.

Finally Ronnie undulated away, then back, presenting me with one hip, on which the bikini bottom was tied. She thrust the hip toward me, and I wasted little time untying the knot. She slid the bottom down and kicked it away. For that moment I was the only one with a good view of my wife's pussy, but gooey hands quickly allowed everyone in the audience to see her neatly trimmed bush and peek at the flesh beneath. Her swollen clit told me she was as horny as I was.

"You know what I want to do now," I whispered. "Is this goo safe for inside you?"

Her grin was wide. "You bet."

As I had done a few times before, I picked Ronnie up and slid her body against mine. She wrapped her legs around my waist and linked her feet in the small of my back. Our size difference makes this position easy for us, so I danced around the stage a few times, then lifted her and impaled her on my shaft. The patrons of the club went wild, screaming and clapping. I couldn't see much beyond the stage, but as I faced the audience, I could tell that several couples were imitating our behavior, either while standing up or sitting in their chairs.

Ronnie threw her head back and clasped her hands behind my neck as I held her tightly. It was as good as it has ever been, fucking her right there on the stage, with dozens of people watching. I wanted to hold back and give them a great show, but my cock wouldn't cooperate. With a loud grunt I came, my penis erupting and filling my wife's pussy with my own personal goo. I think she came as well, but I was too far gone to know. If she hadn't, I'd take care of that later.

We slowly dropped to the wooden floor and someone threw a tablecloth over us as we cooled. "Holy shit," I said.

"I thought you'd like it, but I never anticipated we'd do it, right here."

"Are you sorry we did?" I asked, suddenly worried.

She hugged me close. "Not in the least. Let them all appreciate how good we have it."

"We do have it good, don't we?"

"Hell, yes," she said. "Hell, yes."

My Husband Snores

My husband snores. Loudly. Now I know it's not Steve's fault, but that doesn't make it any easier to deal with when I'm awake at 3 AM and he's making enough noise to wake the dead. Fortunately, most of the time I'm a heavy sleeper and it doesn't really bother me. However, when I'm awake in the middle of the night, for whatever reason, I can't help it. I get mad.

Or I get even. I may be a heavy sleeper but one sound from one of my kids and I'm wide-awake. One night one of the boys woke up with a nightmare and needed a little TLC to get back to sleep. I calmed four-year-old Timmy down, then gave him the flashlight from the kitchen so he could chase away any monsters. "They don't like the light," I told Tim as he snuggled beneath the covers, flashlight at the ready. He tried the beam out a few times and then promptly fell back asleep.

I turned out all the lights, climbed back into bed and listened to Steve's "wood sawing." As I lay there I thought about this and that, then lapsed into one of my favorite fantasies. It's about one of the minor characters, a doctor, in one of those TV crime-scene shows. As my brain wandered, I imagined that I was wounded and his hands were exploring my body to find the injury. *Keep looking,* I thought.

As I lay between consciousness and sleep, I found myself getting aroused. I smiled and wondered whether Steve would stay asleep if I just played with myself a little. That might ease the need and allow me to go back to sleep. For some reason it didn't occur to me to wake him and jump his bones.

I slipped my fingers between my legs. I knew I was swollen and wet and I pressed gently to ease the increasing throb as, in my fantasy, the crime-scene investigator's hands slid over my injured body. I rubbed a little harder, then I considered going into the bathroom and masturbating to orgasm, but at that moment Steve turned over and his snoring worked its way into my mind. He snuffled, then turned on his side facing me and draped his arm over my ribs. Moments later he was breathing noisily and evenly. I cuddled close to his long, lean body, letting his warmth meld with my heat. No bathroom for me. So I stroked my pussy, trying not to move too much and wake my husband.

Then I began to wonder whether I could touch him without waking him. I slowly ran my hand over his flank. When his breathing remained even and noisy, I continued my hand's meandering. I love Steve's skin, so soft, yet firm beneath. His abs are tight, and I found that my fingers could do quite a bit of wandering without disturbing his rest.

I slid my hands over his shoulder, then ran my palm over his collarbone. I knew how good he would smell and taste, so in my now highly aroused state, I moved slightly so I could slide my tongue over his neck. If he woke, fine; if not, fine too.

As I nibbled his neck I thought about how really heavily he was sleeping, and my thoughts turned to his cock. I wondered how hard it would be and how difficult to find out. Was he aware, somewhere deep in his brain, that I was petting him? Would his cock have reacted? I reached down and touched the tip with my finger. Sure enough, he was partially erect. Although he was sound asleep, his body knew what was going on.

I lightly ran my fingertip over his shaft, then wondered how far I could go. I wriggled down beneath the covers and kissed his hard stalk. He mumbled something, then turned onto his back, his breathing still thick and noisy.

Now I had easy access to him, and I took full advantage. I slowly drew his semihard erection into my mouth and sucked gently, my fingers between my legs fondling myself. He grew hard in my mouth. Thinking back on it now, I should have suspected he was playing possum, but it didn't occur to me at that moment. I wanted him so I sucked him like a popsicle. God, I do love his cock. The smell of him can almost make me come, and as I licked and sucked, I continued stroking myself, drawing out my pleasures.

"Enough, Amy," Steve said softly, obviously wide-awake. "You'll get yourself off all by yourself and leave me no fun at all."

Startled, I climbed back up the bed and out from beneath the covers. "How long have you been awake?"

"Actually, since you first came back to bed."

I playfully slapped at him. "You mean you let me get up with Timmy and didn't offer to help?"

I could feel his grin. "You're good at getting him back to sleep quickly, and anyway," he said, sliding his hand down my belly, "I'm offering to help now." He slipped his fingers between my legs and found my clit.

I couldn't be upset. I knew what I wanted from Steve and it wasn't kid tending. I wrapped my hand around his cock, and as he rolled over me, I guided him into my hungry channel. As soon as he was lodged deep inside, I linked my feet behind his back and pulled him as close as I could.

His hand found my breast as his mouth found mine. Now all my delicious spots were being teased. He played me like a musical instrument, driving me higher and higher, while taking his pleasure as well.

I think we both extended it as long as we could, but eventually I felt my climax exploding deep in my belly. "I'm going to come," I moaned.

"Good," he said. "Let it go. Let me feel it." He held still inside of me as orgasm claimed me. My vaginal muscles squeezed his cock and I could feel every twitch of him deep inside. As I came down, I used those muscles to milk his cock, and soon he could take no more.

He pounded into me, stifling his usual groans in deference to the hour. His body stiffened and his back arched. I put my hands on his ass and felt his cheeks contract. Later, as our breathing calmed, he whispered, "That was fabulous."

"I'm understandably amazed at you. I thought you were asleep."

"I know, and I wanted it that way. You were doing the most wonderful things to me, so why interrupt? The hardest part was keeping my breathing even. I guess my snores kept you convinced." He demonstrated with a noisy exhale.

"Actually, the hardest part was this," Amy said, squeezing his now-flaccid cock.

Steve laughed. "Why didn't you wake me? I would have been happy to be an active participant from the start."

"I guess I didn't want to disturb you. And anyway, it was much more fun starting that way."

"You're certainly right about that." He yawned and hugged me close. In only moments he was fast asleep, snoring as usual. Somehow I didn't mind it quite as much and I was soon asleep too. Now I had a good idea of what to do if I awoke again in the middle of the night.

The Power of the Mind

❧

OKAY, I'LL ADMIT IT. I'M A BIT OF A DEVIL AND I LOVE PLAYing the kind of games only someone with my powers can. I discovered long ago that I could move things with the power of my mind. Only little things, I admit, but I can certainly do it. I've honed the ability since I discovered it in my early teens, so now I can make small things obey my will without much effort.

Oh, I know I could make a fortune by forcing dice to roll my way and thus win in any craps game, but that wouldn't be right. I'm a pretty moral fellow. Of course, when I was in high school, I used to play pranks on my friends, but now that I'm in my late twenties I've learned to harness my powers and use them only for my sexual pleasure. And my lady's.

Sexual pleasure. Exactly what do I mean? Let me give you an example.

Last weekend I had a blind date with a new lady, one I'd met through an online dating site. Her profile—if it was accurate— suggested we'd be a great match. We were both well educated and worked in the financial services area. According to her bio, she liked reading mysteries and watching seventies TV cop shows, and miracle of miracles, she loved baseball. She fit me to a tee.

We'd exchanged e-mails and had talked on the phone several times. Things just got better and better each time. She sounded wonderful.

Sensibly, we'd arranged to meet at an Italian restaurant about halfway between our Manhattan apartments, and as I entered, I recognized her immediately from her picture on the website. She was a redhead, with shoulder-length hair, deep blue eyes and freckles. She wasn't beautiful, but then neither am I. Just two average people, me with my strange ability.

"Hello. You must be Amanda." I corrected myself. "I mean, Mandy."

Although she wasn't gorgeous, her smile was warm and extended all the way to her eyes. "Nice to meet you, Kevin. You're right on time." She offered me her hand and we shook. There was a nice sexual tingle that I was sure she felt too. The anticipation was building.

"Actually I was here fifteen minutes ago," I admitted, "but I didn't want to appear overeager."

We laughed, and as we sipped a good bottle of Chianti and talked, we discovered that we had more in common than even the profiles on the site could have predicted. By the end of the meal we were both feeling congenial and relaxed. We were both unattached adults, so eventually the conversation wandered into light sexual banter. When we'd filled out the online questionnaire, we'd both responded that we did, occasionally, have sex on the first date, and now we both suspected where the evening was headed.

So I played a little. I watched her eyes as we talked and used my mind to tighten her bra cups around her breasts. I watched her face flush and heard her breath catch in the middle of a sentence.

I subtly glanced down and could see her nipples tighten into quite obvious buds. I hadn't noticed earlier how large her nips were, and I delightedly realized that she had even more to offer than I had thought at first. I must admit that I'm a devoted tit man.

I put on my most innocent face. "Is something wrong?" I asked.

"I'm sorry. I guess I lost track of the conversation. That doesn't often happen to me."

"No problem," I said, tightening the cups of her bra a little more.

Her flush deepened, and I knew I was getting to her. "I, uh, I think I'd better go to the ladies' room. I'll be right back." As she stood up, I tweaked her nipples with my mind, just for a second.

When she returned several minutes later, her nipples were back to normal. As she sat back down in her chair, I used the power of my mind to slowly compress her breasts again. I saw her swallow hard, and by the flush on her face I could tell she was getting as turned on as I was. I squeezed just a little more, then relaxed my hold on her beautiful tits. "How about going back to my apartment for some coffee or a nightcap?" Tweak.

"I'd love to," she said, releasing a long breath. As she stood, she surreptitiously rubbed her upper arms across her breasts, so I let my mind relax its hold.

We got our coats and took a cab to my apartment building. As we rode up in the elevator, I used my mind to caress her pussy just once with the crotch of her panties. The ease with which it slid over her flesh told me how wet she was. She squirmed and her eyes glazed over for a moment. She was visibly enjoying the sensations.

In the living room of my little flat, I got us each a drink and we settled on the sofa. Quickly the drinks were forgotten as I took her in my arms and brushed my lips across hers. She leaned back on the cushions and slowly wrapped her arms around me. As we kissed,

I tangled my fingers in her hair and tweaked her nipples again with my mind. She wiggled beside me, opened her mouth and snaked her tongue into mine.

The kiss was so deep I couldn't concentrate on her tits, so I just relaxed into it. I heard little purring noises coming from deep in her throat, and a shiver shot through me. I thought of her panties against her wet pussy and stroked, while both my hands were still cradling her head. She moaned. I love it that I can do that to a woman.

I felt my cock harden and fill my shorts. I laid her back onto the sofa cushions and pressed my groin against her pubic bone to relieve the throbbing, but it didn't help. It was as though someone was holding my erection, pumping it. I wriggled a bit and the pressure eased. *Don't be too fast,* I told myself. *Patience.*

We quickly removed our clothes and almost ran into the bedroom. I flipped off the quilt on the bed, and as I started to settle, naked against the sheets, I felt her hand on my cock. But it couldn't be. She had her back to me. She was folding the quilt and putting it on a chair.

"What the hell?" I said.

She turned, a small smile on her face. "We have more in common than you know." The hand tightened on my cock.

"You're doing that with your mind?"

She laughed, a delightfully light sound. "Two can play." The invisible hand expertly stroked my cock from tip to base and back again. Nothing had ever felt that perfect. Then I felt a scratching sensation on my balls and she giggled. It felt wonderful. My cock hardened still more—as if that were possible.

I used my mind to play with her vaginal lips and heard her long sigh. Suddenly it had become a contest: Who could tease whom in what ways without touching? I played with her nipples and she cupped my balls. I pulled at her pussy lips; she rubbed the tender area between my balls and my anus.

I kneaded her ass cheeks, then pulled them apart. She did the same to mine. Then I played with her anus, using my mind to rim her hole, knowing she'd do the same to me. When she did, it was as erotic as anything I'd ever felt. My cock was now so hard that I was beginning to lose the ability to concentrate.

"Me too," she said, grabbing my hand and pulling me onto the bed. I buried my face between her breasts, licking and sucking at her flesh. "The real thing feels better than when you do it with your mind," she said, her voice a soft purr.

"It does indeed." I unrolled a condom over my staff, then held my cock and used the tip to rub her sopping clit. She moaned, and I slid inside. She was so aroused that her pussy was wide-open, and I thrust deeper inside of her than I'd ever been with anyone.

As I thrust, she used her mind and her vaginal muscles to milk my cock, and I used my mind to rub her clit. I thrust, first quick and hard, then teasingly slowly. I inserted only the tip and held it there, then plunged to the hilt. She scratched my back, then bit my small nipples. *No wonder women like it when I do that to them,* I thought.

We played with intercourse for long minutes until neither of us could wait any longer. We came within seconds of each other, long, loud moans filling the air.

Later we lay side by side. "I didn't know anyone else could do that," I said.

"Neither did I, but when I went into the ladies' room and thought about what I'd been feeling, I figured out what you must have been doing. You're pretty good at it too."

I admired her ability. "So are you. You made me crazy."

"I've never done that before. During sex, I mean." She lightly touched my cock with her mind. "But this is dynamite."

"It is that," I said, brushing my mind over her nipples, watching them become erect again. "Feel good?"

"Oh, yes." She sighed as tendrils of her mind swept over my belly. "I'm eager to see what other delightfully naughty things we can do to each other."

I just grinned and mentally fucked her pussy, stretching it to its limits. Fun and games!

Gakked Out

❧

THE AUTO ACCIDENT WASN'T REALLY THAT BAD, BUT MY chest injury was serious enough that the hospital decided I needed to be kept overnight for "observation." Possible bruised lungs and heart—scary, but certainly not life threatening, they assured me. They put me in a small private room with lots of monitoring equipment hooked to me and then got me gakked out on pain medication. Let me tell you, before they gave me the meds, my broken ribs hurt enough that I swore never to drive without my seat belt again. Period.

Sometime in the middle of the night I heard someone enter my room, and opening my eyes, I saw a gorgeous nurse approach with a clipboard. She was tall and slender with long jet-black hair and deep blue eyes. She was built like she was created to match my specifications: adequate breasts with deep cleavage, small waist and slender hips, all of which showed to perfection in the tight little white uniform she wore. Let me tell you, she was like something from a fantasy.

"I'm so sorry, Mr. Meade. I didn't mean to wake you. I just need to get some information from these monitors. Our central computer is giving us a real headache right now. Some kind of transmission glitch or other." Her voice was like a haunting melody and gave me shivers up and down my spine.

"No problem," I said softly, wondering what I could do to make her stick around for a while just so I could look at her. She wrote several things on her clipboard, then took my blood pressure and pulse. Her hands were cool and gentle on my skin, and I was sure that her presence was making my heart race. Fortunately she didn't seem to notice. As she turned to leave, I said, "I'm wide-awake now and it's pretty lonely here. Can you stay for a few minutes?"

"I'm so sorry that I woke you up. You've got your TV, and I'm sure you can find something to amuse you," she said.

"I know, but I'd prefer some real human company."

She looked at her watch, then tucked a strand of that long, sexy hair behind her ear. "Actually you're the last patient I have to see for right now, so I could stay and visit for a short time." She pulled a chair beside my bed and settled into it comfortably. She crossed her legs, and her short skirt allowed me to see quite a bit of soft, white thigh.

I glanced at her name tag. "Ms. Schmidt. You must have a first name."

Her smile lit up the entire room and warmed me deep inside. "It's Jane."

"Well, Jane, tell me a little about yourself."

We talked for several minutes, then I had to sneeze. The pressure on my ribs made me wince, so she pressed a small towel against them to protect them from my second sneeze. Despite my discomfort I noticed that she smelled musky and—I don't know exactly how to put this—sultry. I put the hot aroma out of my mind. "Thanks. That's much better." And the second sneeze was indeed much less painful.

"I'm so sorry you hurt," she said, her voice breathy and, to my ears, erotic. *I must be really out of it,* I thought. Everything about her seemed to scream *sex*. "Would you like me to put some lotion on your chest?"

The thought of her hands on me was so delicious and more than a little arousing, so I almost said no. How embarrassing would it be for me to get a raging hard-on! But the idea was so tempting, so appealing. *Oh, what the hell.* I nodded. "I'd like that."

Jane rummaged in the drawer of my bedside table and found a bottle of skin lotion. She poured a dollop into her palm, then rubbed her hands together to warm it. I closed my eyes and tried to focus on waterfalls. Lots of cold water. Okay, that didn't work. What about hot, sandy, gritty, sweaty deserts? Anything to keep my mind off of her hands. Those long fingers with the deep red polish. No latex gloves for Jane Schmidt.

I kept my eyes closed as she pulled the sheet to my waist and tucked it beneath my hips. She parted the top of my hospital gown and began to slowly smooth lotion on my pecs. I don't have a great body, but she didn't seem to notice. Why should she, after all? This was a totally professional massage.

The slow rubdown was heavenly, and despite all my concentration, my cock slowly stiffened. She expertly massaged my shoulders and neck, then down my right arm to my hand. I never would have believed that rubbing goop over my fingers could be so sensual, but Jane rubbed each finger as though it were my cock, a sensation not lost on my stiffening hard-on.

She moved to the left side of the bed and repeated her ministrations on my other arm and hand. By now it was all I could do to keep my hips still.

"Poor baby," she said finally. "You look like you're in such pain. Should I call someone?"

Call a hooker, I wanted to say, but instead I whispered, "It's okay."

"No, it's not," she purred. "Shall I try to relieve your discomfort?"

My eyes flew open. Was she saying what I thought she was saying? Nah. Couldn't be. It would just be more chest rubs, and I didn't think my cock could stand any more. This was a hospital, after all, not a brothel. "It's okay," I said again.

"I mean," she whispered, gazing at the tent now fully formed over my dick and smiling, "that discomfort."

I kept quiet, hoping but not expecting anything. She brushed the back of her hand over the tented sheet. "I could soothe you so you could go back to sleep."

"If you think it's best," I said in my most neutral voice.

"Oh," she said, "I do." She pulled the sheet down to my feet, exposing my entire body, the lower part now covered only by the thin hospital gown. She slid the palm of her hand over my erection with only a layer of overwashed cloth between me and the warmth of her skin. "This must be getting very painful."

I moaned as her hand glided over me. "Oh, yes," she said. "It's a nurse's duty to make her patient as comfortable as possible." Then she grasped me through the gown and held me tightly. I knew from the little slice of cold that my gown now had a small precome wet spot right over my dick. I moaned again.

"That damp spot must be uncomfortable." She pulled the gown aside fully, freeing my cock, which now stuck straight up from my groin. Her fingers were warm and slippery from the lotion she'd used as they surrounded my shaft and began to jerk me off. "It's okay," she purred. "Just let go."

Not a chance. This was heaven, and I wasn't about to come too quickly. Back to thoughts of waterfalls and deserts. Anything but her hands so expertly manipulating my dick. Lord, she had talented hands.

Then her mouth was on me, her lips tightly pursed around my dick. Her long hair brushed my belly and thighs, erotic and sensual. Deserts be damned. I concentrated on the feel of her lips and her hair. My hips bucked slightly and I couldn't hold back any longer, so I let it happen and released a stream of semen into her mouth. I still had my eyes closed, the more to savor the sensations, so I pictured small dribbles of goo escaping from her reddened lips.

Finally she stood up, pulled my gown and sheet back into place and left the room. I was asleep before the door closed behind her.

The following morning I awoke, feeling decidedly better, both in my ribs and my crotch. I couldn't believe what had happened. I wanted to see that nurse again, if only to say thanks for the "good care" she'd given me. After several nurses came and went, I figured out that she was probably off duty. However, I wanted to at least leave her a note.

After the doctor checked me over and did all the discharge stuff, I was finally in my wheelchair ready to leave. An orderly parked me beside the nurses' station and I finally had a chance to ask about Ms. Schmidt. "Schmidt?" the nurse at the desk asked, looking puzzled. "I don't think we have anyone by that name here. Let me check."

She disappeared into a little room, then returned. She clacked a few keys on her computer keyboard, then shook her head. "I'm sorry. We don't have anyone here by that name."

"No Schmidt? Jane Schmidt?" Suddenly it sounded like Jane Smith. A phony name?

"I'm sorry."

"But I saw her last evening. She came into my room during the night to check on me after some kind of computer glitch."

"I don't know what to tell you, Mr. Meade. There's no one by that name, and we had no computer glitch last evening that I know of." She reached out and patted my hand. "Maybe you just dreamed her."

I thought for a few moments, then said, "Maybe I did." Maybe I didn't. Maybe some nurse didn't want to give me her name. After all, giving out hand jobs definitely wasn't in the nurses' rule book. But I distinctly remember that she wore a name tag. Real or a dream—who cares? It was fabulous either way.

The Pirate

❧

FANTASIES ARE SUCH DELICIOUS THINGS. MY HUSBAND IS out of town so I lie here in bed with only my dreams to keep me company. The wonderful part of this is that here in the dark I'm untroubled with reality. I can be anywhere I want, be anyone I choose. Tonight I choose to be a beautiful English lady, maybe someone distantly related to the Queen, sailing to the New World to be married. I've never met the man I'm going to wed, but I hear that, although he's much older than I am, he's not too bad to look at. I hope so. Since I'm only eighteen, I've got a dream of a handsome, dashing man who will share my life.

This afternoon the sea is glass smooth, the sky a deep azure blue with a few little white, cottony clouds, and the slight breeze is warm on my face. Then there's a shout and seamen start running around the deck. A bearded deckhand quickly hustles me off to my cabin and hands me a pistol. "What's this for?" I ask. "I couldn't shoot anyone."

His laugh is nasty. "If the pirates begin to pound on the door, that's to shoot yourself."

"That's even more ridiculous," I say, but he's already closed and locked the cabin door.

It seems like hours before anything happens, then the noise suddenly becomes horrific. Men yelling, guns booming, swords clashing, I can hear it all through my open porthole. Then someone rattles the door to my cabin. I raise the gun, but I'm pretty sure I couldn't shoot it.

Then the pounding begins. *If the pirates begin to pound on the door, shoot yourself.* Nope, I'm too much of an optimist. Soon the door splinters and from that moment everything happens in fast motion. I'm grabbed and stuffed under the arm of a gigantic, beefy sailor who carries me from my ship across a plank laid from rail to rail over the water and onto the pirate vessel, then drags me below and locks me in another cabin. I kick until my legs ache, scream until my throat is sore, but to no avail. Here I am, locked in, and suddenly exhausted.

I look around my prison cell. The cabin is luxuriously furnished. Except for the fact that everything is bolted to the floor, it could be a room in any fancy manor house, with sturdy chairs, a table, a desk and walls of bookshelves. My eye lights on a soft-looking bed with satin sheets and a thick comforter. Suddenly the events of the day descend on me and I'm even more exhausted. I collapse on the bed and am immediately deeply asleep.

Noise in the cabin brings me back to consciousness, and I slowly turn over and open my eyes. He's tall, well built, clean shaven and dressed in a tight black breeches, high, shiny black boots, a white lawn shirt with full sleeves and black leather gloves. His hair is ebony brown, worn long and tied at the back of his neck with a leather thong.

He strides to the bed and gazes down on me. "Wake up,

Princess. Time to discuss what I'm to do with you." His voice is deep and a bit gruff.

"Put me back on my ship and leave me in peace."

"Sorry, but your ship is long gone, Princess. We took whatever looked appealing and sent them off. They won't return for you."

I try to sound strong but my voice is shaky. "Of—of—of course they will. I'm valuable cargo, and they are being well paid to transport me."

"They think you're dead, or as good as, and when I last saw them they were too frightened to even consider anything else. The question is, should I make their belief a reality or will you be a good girl?"

I try to take a swing at him, slap his handsome, grinning face, but he grabs my wrist and with little trouble gains control of me. He holds me, and when he's sure I will fight no longer, he lets me go. I scramble to the side of the bed nearest the wall. "That's a little better," he says, "but you'd better learn to be nice to me. If not? I could always put you in the hold and let my men take turns with you. After all, we've been at sea for several months."

His men? "You wouldn't." He merely stares. "You c-c-couldn't," I sputter, watching a grin slowly spread across his face. He could and he would. I have no doubt of that.

He waits until the situation sinks in to my brain. "I can see in your eyes that you're starting to understand the difficulty of your situation, Princess. Be nice or don't—it's all up to you." Leering at me, he removes his gloves, finger by finger, and tosses them on the small desk.

I consider my options and quickly come to the conclusion that I have none. Resigned, I sigh. "I'll be nice."

"Smart girl. Now, it's time for dinner, but you're not dressed properly."

I look down at my simple lawn dress with lace at the sleeves and neckline. Not dressed properly? My puzzled expression seems to amuse him, and he chuckles. "Actually you're too dressed. Dinner will arrive soon and we will share it. However, I wouldn't want you to dirty your only dress, since it will have to last for as long as you're on my ship. Therefore, you will eat naked. Take your clothing off. All of it."

"Naked?"

He sits on a mahogany chair and puts his booted feet on the table. "Your move, Princess."

Options? Again I realize that I have none. He's counted on that, and on my eventual acceptance of that fact. "Now?"

"Right now."

I look around the cabin for a screen to use, but there isn't one. Oh God, naked? Undress right here, in front of him? But what's my other choice? The hold, with his men? Not likely. I'll do what I have to do to survive and look for a way to escape when I can. I heave a deep sigh, now resigned to what's to come.

I reach behind me but I cannot open the many buttons that close the back of my frock. Until now I've always had an attendant.

"I understand. I'll play lady's maid," he says, stepping toward me. I feel his warm hands on my flesh as he slowly slips each button from its buttonhole. He deliberately slides the callused pad of his thumb down my spine as the sides of my dress part. "That's better," he says as the dress slips to the floor. "Let me see what I've got." He takes me by the shoulders and turns me to face him.

Dressed only in my camisole and pantelettes, I know he can see most of my body. I try to stand up straight. No man has ever seen me this way and I can feel a blush creep over me.

"You have a beautiful body. This might prove to be fun for both of us."

I strangle on a meaningless protest. Then he grabs the front of my camisole and uses the fabric to pull me to him. He presses his lips against me as he unties the ribbon that holds my undergarment closed. I know that he's going to be able to see my naked body, but his lips are so hot, so enticing, that I close my eyes and lean into him. I can feel the vibration of a growl deep in his throat as he cups the back of my head and buries his fingers in my hair. Pins fly everywhere and my long locks, freed of their knot, tumble down my back.

He grabs the thick fall, wraps it around his hand and uses it to pull my head back, his mouth on my neck, licking and nipping. Finally he withdraws and settles back in the chair. "Let me see the rest of you."

His eyes never leave mine as I stammer, "I c-c-can't."

"You can do anything you want, and you want this. Or rather you don't want the alternative." He crosses his legs at the ankles. "Do it!"

I have no choice. My face flaming, I slowly pull my camisole and stockings off, then my pantellettes follow. I am now as naked as I was the day I was born. I try to cover my breasts and mound with my hands, but the pirate merely laughs.

His expression and his silence say more than words, so I lower my hands. "Lovely," he purrs as his gaze rakes me. "It seems I've acquired quite a prize."

There's a knock at the door and he whisks the cover from the bed, wraps me in it and pushes me into a corner. "It won't do for the men to know what they're missing," he whispers, standing between me and the door. "Come in."

A tall, lanky teenaged boy stands at the door, trying not to be seen looking around the cabin. "Bring it in, Jake." The boy enters carrying a large tray. "Just put it on the table and keep your eyes to yourself." He does, then leaves quickly.

"Hungry?" the captain asks.

I realize that I'm starving. "Yes," I whisper.

"Good. Some honesty for a change." He crosses the cabin and, with one swipe, whips the cover from my body and motions me to a wooden chair. I sit and feel the cold of the wood against my thighs and the flesh between my legs. The height of the table allows him full view of my large breasts as he fills a plate with roasted fowl, potatoes and vegetables. He adds bread and cheese, then puts the plate in front of me and fills another for himself.

I cannot resist the smells, and I eat hungrily while he merely nibbles at his food, watching me. When I've eaten my fill he grins at me. "I love a hearty appetite. Let's hope all your appetites are as lusty."

What can I say? I've given up fighting.

"Some wine?" he asks.

Without waiting for my answer, he fills a glass for each of us. "Let's see how you taste." He rounds the table and pours a tiny bit of red wine on my chest. Drops slowly trickle down my breast until a ruby droplet finds my nipple. He leans down and flicks his tongue to catch the liquid. My nipple contracts as he sucks.

More drops and more flicks of his tongue have me wiggling in my chair. I can't seem to get comfortable. The flesh between my legs is hot and feels wet and swollen. There's an ache deep in my belly.

He pours more wine on the other breast and follows the trickle with his tongue. Then he picks me up and lays me on the bed. Wineglass in hand, he sits on the edge, then pours the cool liquid on my belly. "Princess," he said, "this is going to be so beautiful." He slips a finger between my thighs. "You're soaked already. Although you don't realize it yet, you're all woman." He sucks my juices from his finger, then laps at the wine on my belly. His tongue finds my navel and he dips it into the wine-filled cavity. "Delicious."

He parts my legs and pulls my feet up until they are flat on the bed, heels against my bottom. Now he can gaze at all the secret places that no man has ever seen. Eventually I feel wine poured on my pubic bone and it dribbles into my folds. "Let me lick that too," he whispers.

He uses his hands to part my flesh. For the first time, I protest. "Please. Don't," I whimper. What am I protesting? Though I don't want it to be, the pleasure is intense. That's what I don't want—I don't want to enjoy him. But I do.

"You don't mean that, Princess," he says. One flick of his tongue on my swollen flesh and I know he's right. "Maybe you ought to say that. Tell me it's all right."

I clamp my lips tightly shut. I want to tell him how much excitement he's causing, but I can't. I'm a good girl and this just can't be giving me so much pleasure.

"Say it. Tell me how good it feels."

His tongue is licking me, causing spears of erotic pleasure to course through me. "Tell me, Princess." That tongue. He's driving me crazy. "Tell me or I won't let you get where you want to be."

Where I want to be? Yes. I want something, but I'm not sure what. But he knows, and he won't let me have it until I tell him. "Yes," I breathe. It's no more than a sigh, but he hears me. His mouth covers my mound and he sucks. My back arches and my knees spread farther. *More!* my body cries.

His mouth leaves. "Tell me you want this. Beg me."

"No, I can't."

His fingers find my folds and he plays with me, teasing, tempting, pushing me higher, toward something I don't understand, then leaving me. One finger presses inside of me and I hear my own long moan. "Beg," he says. "Say please."

He's in control of me and I want what I know he can give me. "Please," I whisper.

Then his fingers fill me and his teeth find my nipple. Spasms of unimaginable pleasure echo through my body. He leaves, but only for a moment, then covers my body with his own lean, strong form. His naked cock fills me, my spasms continuing until he bellows his pleasure in my ear.

By now my fingers are between my legs and I climax from the image of my pirate. Later, replete, tired from my climax, I hear the phone ring. "Hello, Princess," my husband says. "Miss me?"

I stretch. "You have no idea how much."

It's Made out of What?

THE PACKAGE MY HUSBAND HAD GOTTEN ME FOR MY BIRTH-day was wrapped in silver paper, tied with a wide red ribbon and topped with a huge bow. As I gazed at the box, Jeff was grinning like the proverbial Cheshire cat. "I think you'll really like it," he said as I slowly untied the ribbon. Very slowly. Actually I love torturing him by taking my time.

"I know I will," I said, carefully folding the wide ribbon and putting it aside. Then I shook the box. "I wonder what it is." I turned it over and shook it again.

Jeff burst out laughing. "You're the very devil, but I can guarantee you'll get yours. Open the fuckin' thing before I rip it out of your hands and open it myself."

Laughing with him, I pulled off the tape and opened the paper, giggling and folding it neatly. The box was plain brown cardboard, held together with more tape. Jeff handed me a pair of scissors and I used it to slash the tape. The top of the box opened, and, nestled inside, wrapped in bubble wrap, was an unusual glass sculpture. "What the hell?"

I unfastened the wrap and pulled it out. The item was clear, heavy glass, long and slender, with swirls of colored paint around the outside. If it was a sculpture it was very odd since it had no base or stand. I rummaged around in the box, but I found nothing else inside.

As I looked the glass object over, turning the cool material in my hands, I suddenly recognized the shape of the tip. It was shaped like a phallus. "Holy shit," I said.

"Holy shit indeed," Jeff said, grinning from ear to ear.

"Is that what I think it is? I've never seen anything like it."

"It is indeed. I saw it in on a website and couldn't resist it. It's as lovely in reality as it was in the photo. We could almost display it in the living room. Almost, but not quite." He slid closer to me on the sofa. "It's got a few tricks up its sleeve too." He kissed me, one of his knee-buckling, earth-shattering kisses that always blows my brains. "The kids are asleep, so how about going into the bedroom and trying it out?"

"Is it safe? I mean, what if it breaks?"

"According to the instructions it's totally safe," Jeff assured me. "It's made of Pyrex, the stuff they make baking pans out of. We just have to take care not to drop or chip it, but for its intended purpose it's harmless. Unless, of course, you consider the effect it might have on your psyche." He leered at me.

"It most certainly is beautiful." Leering back at my husband, I stroked the dildo's length, then dropped my head, ran my tongue over the phallus-shaped tip and gazed at Jeff from beneath my lashes. "Really gorgeous. Looks kind of like you, but cooler and more colorful."

Chuckling, Jeff grabbed my wrist and pulled me toward the bedroom. "Enough teasing, woman."

"Never enough teasing. After all, whose present is it?"

"It's for both of us," he said, closing the bedroom door behind him. "Now take your clothes off and be quick about it," he said, with a twinkle as he strode toward the bathroom with the toy in his hand.

"What are you doing?" I asked, eager to see what the dildo felt like inside me.

"You'll see. I said it had a few tricks."

I gazed at the slender glass wand in his hand as he disappeared into the bathroom. Tricks? What tricks? We had quite a collection of toys, including several varieties of dildo, many with vibrating motors and clitoral stimulators. This was just glass, after all. What could it do? Whatever Jeff was doing in the bathroom, I could be sure it would be erotic. He had such a wonderfully creative mind.

I quickly stripped off my clothes and stretched out on the bed. Thinking about the new toy was already getting me hot. I could feel my pussy swelling and my juices beginning to flow. I heard water running in the bathroom, then it stopped but Jeff didn't reappear. I found the waiting frustrating, both mentally and physically. I wanted to reach between my legs and relieve my itch, but I didn't want to spoil Jeff's fun.

As if sensing my mood, Jeff called from the bathroom, "Just be patient."

"Never my best thing," I called back, "but okay."

Five minutes later, when Jeff returned with two glasses of water and our new toy I was already cooled off. *Have faith,* I told myself. *Jeff's timing is always excellent.*

"Okay," he said, "let's see how this feels."

Holding the phallus, he reached between my legs and stroked my slit with it. "It's warm," I said, immediately just as hot as I had been earlier.

"It is indeed," he said, pushing it into me, filling me with smooth, slick warmth. In and out he thrust, driving me higher. "It took me a while to figure out just how hot would be 'hot.'" He reached out and tweaked one nipple, almost pushing me over the edge. But not quite. Jeff knows me very well indeed. "I guess I figured right."

He played with my pussy for a while, then pulled the dildo out and put it into a glass of water, filling me with two of his fingers instead. Up I rushed, then he let me plateau, just keeping me at a preorgasmic level. Suddenly he reached out, took the dildo and thrust it into me. "Holy shit," I yelled. It was freezing. The glass he'd used was obviously filled with icy water because now the little instrument of torture was really cold. A thought flashed through me. Was this going to bring me down? It didn't. As a matter of fact, it had just the opposite effect. The cold was exciting, powerfully so.

"I see that cold works too," he said, idly playing with the end of the dildo that projected from my body. "That's what the instruction paper said." He twirled it inside me, then pulled it out slightly and pushed it back in. "I could take a few minutes and read it to you."

"A few minutes hell," I said, laughing. "I don't have much patience at the best of times and certainly not right now."

It took only a few moments for the wand to adjust to my body temperature, but my arousal didn't diminish. Then Jeff left it inside while he leaned over me and put his mouth on my clit and tongued my slit. I lay there in heaven. Was I being totally selfish? You bet. Jeff and I have no problem with a lovemaking session being all one-sided from time to time. In the future, one day would be all his, but this one was all mine.

As his hot mouth sucked on my clit, I felt him play with the dildo again. He slowly withdrew it and rubbed it around my sopping flesh. Then it slipped toward my anus. Was he really going to do that? We'd played that way occasionally; sometimes it was exciting and sometimes I truly didn't like it. He hesitated, knowing that I could easily indicate that I didn't want to play, but I thought, *Why not?* I could always call things off if I changed my mind.

Then the wand, slippery from my juices, was sliding around my anus, until Jeff found the right spot and pushed it inside. It was dynamite. Being filled that way was more exciting than I could have imagined. He wiggled it a bit, and between that and the flicks of his tongue on my clit, I came, screaming. Several minutes later I was regaining my equilibrium, my breathing slowing and my heart no longer threatening to leap out of my chest. "Holy shit."

"Holy shit is the least of it. I'd say you enjoyed your new present."

"*Enjoyed* is much too small a word for what I just felt. That's the best present you've ever gotten me."

"I found several other things I thought I might order from the same website."

"Great. I love new toys." I reached over to where Jeff lay beside me and squeezed one of his cheeks. "And next time it's my turn to play."

The Pool Guy

⁂

WHAT A CLICHÉ. THE OLDER WOMAN AND THE POOL GUY. Well, I guess it's a cliché because it's so delicious to think about. At least it always has been for me. I've been married and divorced twice and I know what good sex is, at least for me, and have had that and more in my life. Sadly, not right now. Anyway, sitting here in Meg's backyard beside the magnificent pool while she and her husband are at work just makes my fantasy feel more real.

Okay, here's how it works. The pool guy is nineteen and a little geeky, with thick glasses and a body that's still all elbows and knees. In the past, many of my fantasies were built around a gorgeous guy, with washboard abs and a lean, muscular body, a handsome face with dimples. I love dimples. In the past few years, however, I've found that looks matter less and less. It's more the direct, appreciative gaze that says *horny* that lures me.

In this fantasy the guy isn't the type who would attract lots of admirers and that appeals to me. I want to be his first teacher.

Okay, back to the pool. I'm sitting in a lounge chair beside the sparkling water, and he arrives with his chemicals. Bending, testing, vacuuming, emptying the skimmers, he's tempting me without realizing it. God, I love innocence.

"Excuse me, ma'am," he says to me. "Would you mind moving your chair? I need to get to the filter."

"It's Martha, and you don't have to be in such a hurry, do you?" Okay, it's corny dialogue, but in my fantasy, as in real life, I'm not great at come-on lines.

"I'm really sorry, ma'am, but I've got a job to do," he says. Then something in my gaze makes him stop and say, "But I have a few minutes. My name's Joe."

He sits on a chair beside me and we talk about nothing special for a few minutes. Then I ask, "Got a girlfriend?"

"Sure," he says, then he looks sheepish and admits, "Well, not right now."

I glance at his beige shorts and in that department he's not geeky at all. He really fills out the khakis. "So, Joe, have you ever wanted to learn a little more about sex?" In reality I would never have the nerve to say something like that, but, again, this is my fantasy.

He stammers. "W-w-well . . ."

I reach over and touch the rapidly growing bulge in his shorts. "I think you're interested. Why don't you move over and sit on my chair so I can show you a few things?" I pat the lounge chair beside my stretched-out legs.

"I'm not sure this is a good idea."

"Why not? You want to learn, don't you?"

He stares at his feet, obviously considering, then makes a decision. He moves over and sits beside my thighs. "Maybe just about kissing," he says sheepishly.

I use my index finger to guide his chin closer, then softly kiss his lips. He grabs the back of my head to deepen the kiss. "Whoa," I say. "Gently. Don't rush things."

I nibble at his lips and he quickly gets the idea. Gently he rubs his lips against mine, and I slowly open my mouth, letting his seeking tongue inside. Again he's overeager so I pull back. He sighs and smiles. "Teach me," he says.

For long minutes we kiss and he begins to appreciate the enjoyment of a long, lingering kiss. Mouths and tongues play and tease, then my hands cup his face. I stroke his still-soft cheeks with my thumbs and he follows suit.

I lean back. "Hands are all important in lovemaking. Take off your shirt and let me show you." He does, and I stroke his hairless chest, his shoulders, relishing his smooth skin beneath my fingertips and palms. I indicate the tender spot beneath my ear, and the one where my neck and shoulder meet. "These are wonderful places to kiss and lick. Try it."

Shivers ripple down my spine as he does. I can feel my pussy moisten. Next lesson. "Breasts are great to fondle. Do you enjoy a woman's breasts, Joe?"

"Yes." He sighs, staring at my cleavage. His gaze is so tender, so reverent and yet so hungry, that I almost laugh.

I untie my bikini top and let my breasts spring free. Spring? In reality they droop a bit, but in my dreams I can be anyone I want, looking any way I want. I lift my tits and say, "Stroke. Just like kissing, gently and tenderly does it."

He may be a little geeky, but he's got great hands, with long, slender fingers and blunt, smooth nails. As he strokes my flesh, I watch his hands and my already swollen nipples tighten. "See what you do?"

"Oh, yes," he moans. "I want to suck them."

"Do it, but remember what I showed you about starting gently and building from there."

He uses his lips and tongue to tease my nipples. God, he's a fast learner. My back arches in response as he cups one tit and softly sucks the tip into his mouth. I love breast play and I let him fondle and suck for a long time, but eventually my hot, hungry body becomes impatient. I slide my fingers beneath the waistband of his shorts. "Take these off. It's time for the next lesson."

He removes his shorts and his hard cock almost jumps from its confinement. "Now take the bottom of my suit off, again easily and slowly. Tease about it."

He's a little awkward, but gradually my pussy is revealed and I can see the stark hunger in his eyes. I'm not sure be believes yet that he's going to get to enjoy my body, but I know he will—and so will I. "Want to explore?"

"Really?" He's stunned that he's gotten this far and is being invited to go still further.

"Of course. Have you ever played with a pussy and watched your fingers while you did it?"

A long exhalation and slight head shake is his answer.

"Take your time. It's really arousing for me too."

He uses his fingertips to delve into all the wet, slippery crevices. I'm so wet I can feel my juices dampening my thighs. I want his big cock inside me, but the role of teacher is so erotic that I'm reluctant to let it go. "You can slide your finger inside if you like." Like? He is wonderfully eager, and I am so hot I am afraid I'll climax before his hard and ever-so-eager cock is inside me. Would that be so bad?

His finger snakes into my pussy, quickly followed by another. I can barely breathe and my pulse pounds in my ears. "You can make me come." I see his face fall and I grin. "Don't worry–you'll be satisfied too eventually. I promise. If you taste my juices and lightly flick my clit with your tongue you'll be able to share my orgasm." How I'm able to speak in full sentences I've no idea. I part my pussy lips and show him where to lick and he does, with his fingers still pushing inside me.

I come! Waves and waves of pleasure throb through me. "I can feel it," he whispers. "On my fingers."

"See what you can do? How about feeling it on your cock now?"

It's my fantasy and condoms are unnecessary, so he quickly kneels between my thighs and slides his hard, pulsing cock into my still-hungry pussy. He fills me so full that I begin to climax again. He can't wait and I feel his hips buck as his cock empties into me.

WELL, THAT'S MY FANTASY. NOW THAT I'VE BEEN DREAMING it, sitting beside Meg's pool, it's made me feel bereft. I want . . .

"Excuse me, ma'am, but I need to get to the filter."

I open my eyes. The pool guy's here, in all his geeky glory. Hmm. Hmm indeed.

Panty Hose

❧

PANTY HOSE. IF THERE WAS EVER AN INVENTION THAT AN-
noys men and pleases women, it is panty hose. They annoy men
because they discourage, even interfere with, sex, and they please
women because they are easy to put on, eliminate the uncomfortable garter belt and make wearing panties unnecessary—an added
bonus when dressing in slinky clothing: *Voilà!* No panty lines.

My husband, Josh, and I were going to a party with lots of
friends from his office, and I had bought a new dress for the occasion, a teal blue knit with a tight bodice that accentuated my
average-size breasts and a short skirt that showed off my great legs,
to me my best feature. Of course, I was going to wear panty hose
to eliminate any lines and squish whatever extra bulges I have in
my ass and thighs. I knew Josh wouldn't be happy. He loves to
look at me, and that look he gives me, the one that says, "I'm going
to fuck your brains out when we get home," makes me all gooey
inside. But he doesn't give me that look when he knows I'm wearing panty hose.

I was chatting with my sister Sandy on the phone earlier that week and the subject of panty hose came up. She told me she had done a deliciously daring thing several times and it had infused a new spiciness into her sex life that had lasted for weeks afterward. When she gave me the details I decided it might work for Josh and me.

I'm not often particularly brave in the bedroom, or out of it, for that matter, but the more I thought about Sandy's idea, the more excited I became, so I decided to take action. I bought a new pair of control-top hose, and when I got home and opened the package I looked them over. Yup. Just as I'd hoped, they had a knit-in cotton crotch. So I cut it out. There were seams on either side so, when I pulled, the stockings didn't run. Great. I was going to see what my husband thought of them, just before the party. Ain't I the erotic one?

Josh had decided to take his little two-seater sports car that evening, and we drove across town with the top down. It was early fall so I wasn't wearing a coat, just the new dress, a bra, hose and shoes. As we parked in the driveway at his friends' house, I let my skirt ride up really high. "I've got a little surprise for you," I said, putting his hand on my slippery, hose-covered thigh. Then I helped my dress slide up my hips.

"Damn it, Elaine. You know how I hate those things," he said, sounding frustrated. "Don't tease."

With a look of total innocence on my face, I said, "Who, me?" I guided his hand between my thighs and I felt his fingers find my wet core. The look on his face was priceless. "What the hell . . . ?"

I merely smiled, pulled his hand away and opened the car door. As we rang our friends' doorbell, Josh hissed, "Those things have no crotch."

"Right you are," my brave self said with a slight leer, "and you've got all evening to think about it. Every time you glance over and see me, remember that there's nothing between your fingers and my pussy but air." The look on Josh's face was priceless.

Throughout the evening, whenever I glanced at Josh and found him watching me, I winked at him. Oh, he'd gotten the message loud and clear, and I knew from the bulge in the front of his slacks that he wanted to get it on as much as I did. Midevening, I went upstairs to find the bathroom. Ladies, I've never appreciated the old-fashioned split crotches that I've read about in romance novels until the moment when I realized that I could just pull the sides of the hose-crotch apart and pee without having to yank the damned stockings down and wriggle into them again afterward. Maybe those ladies of bygone years had it right.

Anyway, I was walking back down the hallway toward the stairs when I saw Josh coming up. He looked around, and seeing no one, he grabbed me and pressed his chest against mine. "I've been watching your lovely ass all evening," he murmured into my ear, "and thinking about those stockings." He backed me against a wall and slid his hand up the front of my thigh, pushing my skirt up. Then his fingers found me and flicked across my inner lips the way he knows will drive me wild. Back and forth his fingers moved, causing me to buck my hips and make slightly embarrassing noises deep in my throat. I stopped a loud moan but worried that someone might hear the noises I might make if I came.

I needn't have worried. "That's enough for right now," Josh said, pulling away and smoothing my skirt back down in the front. A quick kiss and he was heading back downstairs with a wink that said, "Two can play at your sexy game." I followed him down the stairs and rejoined the partyers, my pussy twitching and frustration flooding my body. A few minutes later Josh wandered up behind me, pressed the swelling in his crotch against my ass and whispered, "Do you feel a migraine coming on?"

You don't have to hit me with a two-by-four. I squinched my

eyes and rubbed my forehead while Josh looked around for our host and hostess. He quickly made our excuses and we headed for our car, which, luckily, wasn't blocked in. He almost peeled rubber as he pulled out of the driveway, and in just a few minutes he had pulled into the darkened parking lot at the local elementary school. "I can't wait," he said, shifting into park and shutting off the engine and lights.

Then his fingers were in my crotch. That wasn't as easy as you think, what with the gearshift, console and all, but I guess he was as hungry as I was. Phew, that's an understatement. Almost immediately two of his fingers were inside me. No breast play, no kissing, no nothing. And I loved it. I wasn't in the mood for foreplay either. I reached across the console and unzipped his pants, then, through the fly of his briefs, I found his cock, hard, hot and ready to go. But go where? Not in the front seat of the tiny car, and there was no backseat. "I guess we'll have to wait until we get home?" I asked, disappointment obvious in my voice.

"Not a chance. I want it right here," he growled. "You're not teasing me anymore." He rammed his fingers in and out of my pussy.

"I want it now too," I giggled, then slapped at his hands, "but don't get too grabby." I pushed his hands away. I was in as much of a hurry as he was, but I also loved the heat and feelings of urgency, and I wasn't ready to let those go just yet. I also enjoyed Josh's excitement. I wriggled around and grasped his erect cock and stroked, holding on tightly. I ran my fingers down the length of his shaft. As one hand reached the base, I started the same procedure with the other. It was as if he were fucking a never-ending pussy.

Precome oozed from the tip and moistened my hand, making the stroking slipperier. I inhaled the fragrance of his heat, loving how hot he had gotten, just from wanted to fuck me. How fabulous!

Panting, he said, "I don't think I can take that much longer."

"Sure you can," I said. I circled the base of his cock with my thumb and forefinger and tightened my grip, forming a sort of cock ring. I'd done this for him several times when we first started having sex, but I'd forgotten about it until now. I knew it would prevent him from coming before I had a chance to play a little more.

I'd love to be able to wrap my lips around him, but no matter how I wriggled it was just impossible in the confined space. Keeping my encircling fingers tightly around the base of his erection, I cupped his sac and played with his balls within.

I could tell by his cock's twitching that he was really close. "Not yet," I said, eager to feel his hands back on me. I let him come down a little before releasing my tight hold on his erection. "I want you," I said, "so very much." We moved around in the tiny space, hoping we could find a position that would allow him to fuck me right there. No dice!

Suddenly he laughed. "I don't think we can manage it in here," he said.

"Maybe we can't fuck, but I need you." I had ended up facing him on my seat, so I guided his hand back to the opening in my panty hose. "God, touch me." His hands rubbed and his fingers thrust, pushing me higher and higher. Let me say that Josh knows me pretty well. He can tell just how to touch me and where. So he did, while I leaned forward and massaged his cock. It was like when we were teenagers. He filled my pussy with his fingers and used his thumb to stroke my clit. I held his cock in one hand and squeezed, alternating my fingers so it felt like I was milking him.

It didn't take long for me to come, my body thrashing in the tiny seat. I tried not to scream, but a few yells were inevitable. As I calmed and my breathing slowed a little, I continued masturbating him until, with a bellow, he came too. I used both my hands to catch his semen, trying not to spill it all over him, his slacks and the car. As he collapsed against the driver's side door, I started to laugh. It was so wonderful, so spontaneous, so incredibly hot.

As he lay there, he joined my laughter. "God, it hasn't been like that in quite a while," he said, panting between words.

"Not in a long time," I said, wiping my hands on a tissue.

"I love panty hose, you know."

Our laughter got louder. "Me too. God, yes, me too. But I could learn to hate tiny little sports cars."

Four

ᴹARGE AND HARRY McKAY MOVED INTO THE HOUSE
down the block from us, and we hit it off almost immediately.
Harry was of medium height, well built, with salt-and-pepper hair,
deep blue eyes and a matching full beard and mustache, which,
taken all together, made him look like a college professor. He was
actually a CPA, and the professorial look probably gave his clients
lots of reassurance, even when faced with a tax audit.

Marge was short, pretty in a June Cleaver sort of way, with
deep auburn hair that probably had help from Lady Clairol and an
open, friendly face that caught my attention when we crashed carts
in the supermarket. My husband, Dan, who was with me at the
time, said she looked comfortably sexy, whatever that meant.

We had them over for dinner a few days later and they quickly
returned the favor. We got very close, very quickly, and within a
few weeks it was as though we'd been friends forever.

One evening about a month after we met, our relationship
changed. It was warm midsummer twilight and we were sitting in

the McKays' backyard, having finished a great barbecue dinner. I was working on my third beer and feeling quite mellow when Harry asked me, "Have you and Dan ever played with another couple?"

My eyes snapped opened. "No." I was shocked that Harry could even ask. "Of course not."

Dan got defensive. "Don't be silly. We've been totally monogamous for all our married life."

"That's a shame," Marge said, patting Dan's hand across the redwood table. "So boring."

I hadn't even suspected that these nice, rather ordinary folks might have done anything that outrageous. "Do you mean you've, well, cheated?" I asked.

"Not at all," Harry said, his expression surprised. "We've never done anything that the other didn't know all about in advance." He took Marge's other hand. "Marge and I have a totally open relationship." His wife nodded in agreement.

"I've heard all about that. Swinging, other partners. I couldn't do that to Paula." Dan slid his hand from beneath Marge's, took mine and squeezed. "I love her too much to risk our relationship."

"Sure, we've had other partners," Harry said, "but I've never done anything behind Marge's back, never lied to her. We know several other couples, friends of ours, who enjoy having sex more, well, let's say more freely, than many. I was just wondering whether you two might want to consider being with us like that some evening." He leaned over and talked directly to me. "I find you quite attractive, and I know Marge has said the same about Dan."

"You mean you've talked about us—that way?" I pictured them discussing our sex life over coffee or in bed. The idea didn't sit well at all.

"Sure. Why not? We're all adults. Do you mean you never had sexual thoughts about us?"

"Of course not." Actually I had. Harry was not handsome, but his charm made him desirable. I had fallen asleep several evenings wondering what he might be like in bed.

"Liar," Marge said, laughing. "But that's okay. You can lie to yourself all you want."

Harry draped his arm around his wife's shoulder. "We all try to attract members of the opposite sex. That's why we humans dress the way we do, use makeup, get nice haircuts."

"We're just saying," Marge said, "that you and Dan have been successful, at least as far as Harry and I are concerned. We're attracted."

"I never tried to be," I protested.

Dan contradicted me. "Of course you did. You take more time dressing to come over here than you would to go to the movies, just us. What's wrong with that?"

I hated to admit it, but he was right, though I didn't think he'd noticed. It embarrassed me, however, to get caught. I dropped my chin and said, softly, "Nothing, I guess." Was there?

"Paula, I'm so sorry," Harry said. "I didn't mean to upset or embarrass you, and I'm sorry I brought the whole thing up. Let's forget all about what I said."

Marge quickly changed the subject and the rest of the evening passed without any further mention of swinging. But it was the elephant in the room and I was sure it was on everyone's mind.

Later that evening, Dan and I had particularly great sex, after which he said, "Did what Harry said interest you the way it did me? I don't want you to think that I was thinking about Marge when we made love tonight, but I have to be honest and say that I've been thinking about their relationship all evening."

I chuckled. "If we're being honest, I have been too. They seem so happy, like the ideal couple. The fact that they have sex with other partners blew me away. I never even suspected."

Dan rolled onto his back, stacked his hands beneath his head and gazed at the ceiling. "Have you ever thought about making love to someone else? Be honest now."

I hesitated. Of course, I'd thought about other men, movie stars, guys I see around the neighborhood, including Harry, even a new sales rep that we'd just hired at work. "I guess I have." The vision of the sexy guy on *CSI* flashed through my head. Him too. I have an active fantasy life, but I'd never considered any of it ever coming true.

"Me too. In my opinion anyone who says he or she doesn't is lying. It's natural to have sexual thoughts about other people. I've never considered acting on them, however."

"Me neither," I said quickly.

"But with Marge and Harry it's suddenly a possibility. Would you consider it?"

"I don't know. I need some time to chew on it."

"Sure." He kissed me deeply, then as we cuddled, spoon style, I felt him fall asleep. I thought about the idea of swapping with Harry and Marge, and I had to admit to myself that the image of being with Harry excited me. But what about Dan and Marge? I trusted him completely and knew that his love for me was powerful and complete. Could I deal with the idea of him with another woman? The more I thought about it, the more the idea aroused and frightened me.

Dan and I didn't get time to talk without the kids around until late the following evening. "I've been thinking about what Harry and Marge said and I'm really curious. How do you feel about it?" I asked.

"I guess I'd like to try," Dan admitted.

"I worry about what happens if it doesn't work out."

We talked for over an hour and agreed to bring it up with our friends the following weekend. It was raining that Saturday so we were lounging in the living room at their place. We had originally planned to get together at our place, but we'd changed at the last minute. Had we moved the evening to the McKays' house since their kids are off at college and their house is empty?

"We've been thinking about what you said last week," Dan said to the other couple after an hour of small talk. "Have you ever lost friends, you know, swinging friends, when things didn't work out?"

Marge answered, "We've occasionally run into situations like that, and in one case we didn't see the couple again after our first evening together."

"But, honey," Harry continued, "we weren't really close to them even before that night so it was no great loss. We've never had to stop seeing another couple we were as close to as we are to you folks because of that kind of thing." He looked at me. "May I surmise that you two might be interested?"

"We just might," Dan said.

Harry's smile was immediate. "That's fabulous."

"It makes me really nervous," I said.

"Good. A little nervous tension only makes it sweeter when it happens." He refilled my beer glass, then put a CD in the player. "Let's dance."

I took a big swallow of beer for courage. *I want this,* I thought, but still my knees shook.

"Let's get one thing clear," Marge said. "Any one of us can call anything off at any time, no hard feelings. Agreed?"

We all agreed. Somehow that made me feel better. I had an out and hopefully there would be no consequences. Harry took me in his arms. The music was sweet and good for slow dancing. Harry was a good dancer, holding me close and guiding me around the living room floor, then into the hallway and then to the dining room.

It felt less scary not being in the same room as Dan and Marge. My heart was pounding, both from excitement and nervousness. Harry's first kiss eased my nerves. His lips were soft and undemanding. It was as though he was giving me every opportunity to pull away. I didn't.

I hadn't kissed another man since Dan and I had married fifteen years before. I'd dreamed, of course, but this was for real. Harry's light kisses moved across my cheeks and down my neck. His fingers stroked my face and slid into my hair. I slipped my hands up his chest to the back of his neck, and I held him as he nibbled at my collarbones through my tee shirt.

Then our lips locked again. This kiss was less tentative, more needy for both of us. "I've been dreaming about this," he whispered, his breath hot against my mouth. "I wondered whether you'd be as soft and sweet as I hoped. You're better." Again his lips took mine. I was relieved that I had only to follow his lead.

He pulled back, lifted my hand to his mouth and turned it palm up. He licked small circles into my palm with the tip of his tongue that made me shiver with delight and expectation. His chuckle was warm. "First times are always special, more exciting because of the delightful anticipation."

He led me into a guest bedroom at the back of the house. "I'd like to see you," he said, again giving me the opportunity to say no. Not a chance. I was too far down this unfamiliar but delicious path to turn back now. I pulled my tee shirt over my head, then let my shorts fall to the floor.

He laughed as his gaze roamed my body. "Do you always wear such succulent undies or did you dress with this in mind?"

Had I? I don't have a great body, but I'd selected my sexiest lingerie, a white lace bra with pale pink roses embroidered over the center of the cups, and matching tiny bikini panties. I felt myself blush with both embarrassment at being caught and with the heat of Harry's gaze.

Harry stripped to his briefs and cupped my breasts. "You're so hot," he said. "I couldn't get the picture of you like this out of my mind all week."

"I thought about you too," I admitted. It hadn't taken much for me to picture him naked. After all, we'd been in our pool together many times. However, despite a slight paunch, his almost naked body had now taken on an erotic aura. And his excitement was obvious.

I started to compare his body with Dan's, then stopped myself. No comparisons of any kind. This would be a stand-alone encounter, good or bad on its own merits. I moved closer and held him to me, feeling his body against mine. As his hands massaged my back, he unhooked my bra and we let it fall to the floor.

Somehow I wasn't worried about my droopy breasts or well-padded belly. This had already moved beyond that. His mouth found mine again and his hands moved to my ass. He kneaded the flesh there, pressing my mound against his hardness. It was exhilarating. I was high and hot and reveling in it.

We separated and finished undressing, then I settled on my back on the bed. Harry knelt beside me and kissed my abdomen. I giggled as his beard and mustache tickled my skin. "Ah, ticklish," he said, rubbing his coarse facial hair against me.

"A little," I said, squirming.

"Good or bad?" he asked.

"Both," I answered. I'd never liked being tickled, but having his face against me was exciting too.

"How about this?" His mouth moved to my mound and his tongue quickly found my erect clit. Flicks of his tongue sent flames of searing pleasure through me. "Good or bad?"

"Very good," I said, almost unable to draw breath into my lungs.

"And this?" he asked, fingers probing my opening. Then he was inside of me, one slender finger playing my clit like an instrument.

"Very, very good," I gasped out.

"You're so wonderfully sensitive," he purred. "This is better than any imaginings, and it's difficult for me to be patient."

"Then don't be." Had I actually said that, invited him to penetrate my body? "You can be patient another time." Would there be another time? Who knew yet?

He rapidly found a condom and unrolled it onto his large cock. Then he covered me with his body, his erection unerringly finding my opening and thrusting inside.

It was ecstasy and I couldn't hold back my climax. It grew from low in my belly, finally taking over my entire body. I wrapped my legs around his waist and held on as my hips bucked. "Oh God, oh God, oh God," I said through clenched teeth, not wanting to scream too loudly.

I felt his ass muscles clench and his back arch as he came.

I was worried that afterward things would be awkward, but they weren't. We dressed and wandered into the kitchen to refresh our beers. We found Marge and Dan seated at the kitchen table with bowls of ice cream.

"Good idea," I said, helping myself from the freezer.

"Regrets?" Marge asked. "Anyone?"

"Nope," Dan said, "at least not now."

"Me neither," I said, "but I don't know how I'll feel when the excitement wears off."

"We'll see what the next week brings," Harry said, a smile in his voice. "Let's talk in a few days and discuss where we want to have dinner next week."

"We'll call you," Dan said. "And dinner next week sounds fine, with or without."

Harry and Marge held hands. "Good. With or without."

Four: Afterward

It was still raining as Dan and Paula left the McKays' after their unusual evening, so Dan pressed the unlock button and the two dashed for their Chevy. Once inside Dan started the engine but didn't put the car in drive. He had questions that wanted answers. "What was it like?"

"I don't know how much we should say about the evening," Paula said. "Although you know I love you, this feels more personal and private and I sort of want to keep it to myself."

"Yeah, I feel that way too, but I'm also really curious. Let's settle on this one question. Was it good?"

The smile on his wife's face said it all. "Yeah," she said. "It was very good."

Better than me? Dan wanted to ask, but didn't dare. "Mine too."

Paula turned to him in the darkened car. "I decided one thing tonight," she said. "No comparisons. I think that would be a great mistake in this whole thing. No wondering 'Was it better with him than with you?' or vice versa. It was something totally separate.

It was hot, as first times are, and that's that. It doesn't have to be one person or another, you or Harry. It can be both."

Dan heaved a sigh. "You're always so sane, Paula, and I think you're right. Marge was wonderful and so are you. Totally different and that means comparisons have to fail. Okay?"

"More than okay." She leaned over and kissed him deeply. "I love you, you know."

"I do know. And I love you." Dan put the car into drive and headed down the block to their house. Marge had been wonderful, sexy as hell and totally different from Paula. She felt different, smelled different, tasted different. It had been terribly exciting. He thought back as he pulled into the garage.

They'd been dancing when Harry and Paula had disappeared into the dining room. He'd had a twinge of worry, but then Marge had whispered in his ear. "We're going to have quite a time tonight."

His cock had reacted immediately. "I guess so." *What if I fail at the last minute?*

"Don't guess. I know so. Let's go inside and play."

They entered a guest room. "Harry and I have a deal. No playing in our bedroom, so I hope this is okay."

"That's a very good idea." He leaned down to kiss her. While Paula was of average height, Marge was tiny and barely came up to his chin. Where Paula was slender, Marge was voluptuous, with large breasts and ample curves. When they kissed he had to lean down to reach her.

With no hesitation she pressed herself against him, snaked her arms around his neck and returned his kisses with gusto. "Mmm," she purred, "I think kissing is the best part of sex."

"Me too," he said, not sure he believed that. He liked to get to it.

Marge rubbed her belly against his hardening dick, and Dan was relieved. No problem there. "I think this baby wants to come out and play," she said, squeezing his cock between her palms. She quickly unzipped his jeans and parted the fly of his briefs. Her hand on his cock was heaven, and he sucked in air and gasped. Other than Paula no one had touched him there in fifteen years.

"Ooo, your baby is quite something. I'll bet he's ready for a real workout. Why don't you get undressed?"

He didn't think but instead pulled off his clothing and dropped everything on a chair. Marge was wearing a tank top and light-weight full skirt, and she seemed to have no intention of taking anything off. He was a little puzzled. "You'll see," she said, sensing his question. "Now lie down. I like to ride my men for a while. That is if you don't mind."

Mind? He was more than willing. However she wanted to play this, as long as he got his cock into her sweet pussy, it was fine with him. Actually, since Paula never wanted to be on top, this would be different and really hot.

He lay on the silky bedspread, cock sticking straight up. "I don't want you coming too quickly," Marge said, reaching into a drawer beside the bed and pulling out a piece of what looked like rubber tubing and a familiar foil packet. She wrapped the elastic strip around his cock and balls and fastened it tightly, then covered his dick with the condom. He'd never used a cock ring before, but it certainly did increase the size and hardness of his package. Not bad. No worries about performance for him.

"Now things won't go too fast." With obvious enthusiasm she climbed over him, crouched above his thighs and lowered herself onto him. No panties. Wow! Then she spread her skirt over their joined bodies. "I love the idea of secret stuff going on beneath my clothes."

Using her strong thigh muscles she levered herself up, then slid her sopping pussy onto him again. Head thrown back, hands playing with her tits, she raised and lowered herself over and over.

His cock ached, swollen and almost painful, needing to come, yet unable to because of the ring around his dick. Watching this tiny woman bounce on his erection, hands kneading her own generous tits, was incredible. She suddenly pulled her shirt over her head and unfastened her bra, then threw both articles of clothing across the room.

Now her fingers pulled at her nipples. Then she leaned forward, grabbed his hands and used them to cup her breasts. He wasted no time and pinched her nipples and squeezed a handful of breast flesh. "Harder," she said, and he dug his fingertips into her softness.

"Yes," she said, panting, bouncing, making low growling sounds deep in her throat. "God, yes. Like that. Just like that."

With one hand he reached beneath the skirt still covering them and found her clit. He massaged it lightly and again she said, "Like that, but harder."

He pressed harder and she came, driving her mound firmly against his groin. She released the fastening on the cock ring and he came hot and hard, pounding into her, spurting more semen than he thought possible, so much, in fact, that some of it trickled onto his hand. He flipped her onto her back, then banged into her over and over until they were both completely spent.

Now, coming back to the present, he opened the car door for Paula. Silent, each lost in thought, the couple ran through the drops to the front door, said good night to their teenaged sons and ran up to their bedroom. "I'm still aroused," Paula said softly as she stopped in the middle of the bedroom. "Or maybe again. I want to make love with you."

Dan nodded. "Me too. Some say that this kind of thing makes sex between old married folks like us better. What say we find out?"

"Think the kids noticed our rush?" Paula asked.

"If they ask, we'll tell them we were merely wet from the rain and wanted to dry off."

"I'm wet," Paula said, now smiling, "but it has nothing to do with the rain." She pulled off her shirt and shorts. "I need a shower first, however. I don't want to smell of anyone else when I make love with you."

"Good thought. Last one to the shower is a rotten egg."

As Paula adjusted the temperature of the spray, she said, "I'm worried that something that happened before will sneak into our bedroom. Maybe some new technique or something. How will that feel? Will you be jealous?"

"I've no problem with doing new things. How about you?"

"I'm okay with anything we do together, wherever it comes from."

He climbed into the stall shower and pulled his wife in beside him. "How about this?" He grabbed the soap, worked up a lather and smoothed his hands over Paula's chest. Slowly he swirled his fingers over her skin until she was covered with bubbles. "Now me," he said, "but this way." He used her soapy chest to massage his, covering them both with froth as they stood beneath the cascading water.

Paula soaped her hands and massaged Dan's back, working her way down to his ass.

"Gotta get all clean," Dan said after a few minutes. Again he soaped his hands, parted her thighs and rubbed lather over her outer lips. Their shower was a handheld model, so he lifted it from its bracket and turned the control to a pulsing stream. Then he focused it onto her pussy. Her low moan told him it was having the desired effect.

He waited until her hips were moving, then handed her the shower. She winked, then turned it on his cock and balls. She rubbed her other hand over the soap and cupped his sac. "Just getting you all clean," she said with a giggle.

"I can't wait much longer to be inside you," he said, needing to devour his wife.

"We can take care of that." She turned off the water and pulled the curtain open. Then she lay down on the thick bath mat and Dan covered her, thrusting his dick into her swollen pussy.

It took him only a few thrusts to climax, then Paula moaned, "I'm going to come."

Her hips bucked and she grabbed his cheeks and held him tightly against her. "Yes. Oh, yes." Since he had come so quickly, he was able to hold still and feel the spasms that rocked her channel.

Later, in bed, Paula said, "I didn't think I could come again so quickly."

"Well, you certainly did and it was wonderful."

"It was indeed. Is this all because of what happened earlier, I wonder?"

"Who cares?" Dan responded. "What happened before was great, but we just made great love. What could be better?"

"Should we do it with them again next week?"

"Why don't we just let it flow? If it happens, fine. If not, that's all right too. I'm good with it either way."

Paula purred and held him close. "Me too. And if nothing else, it's been quite an education."

Beneath the Surface

※

I'VE BEEN WATCHING EROTIC FILMS WITH MY WIFE, BEV, for several months, ever since I discovered an online source for X-rated movie rentals. About once a week, usually late Saturday evening after we come home from whatever we've been doing, we settle in the bedroom and put in a DVD. I have to admit that most of them are trash, just come shots and no story, but occasionally we find one worth watching. A bit of wheat among the chaff.

One particular evening we were watching one. The idea was nonsense, of course, about a lingerie model who gets involved with a customer. The plot, such as it was, was silly, lots of naked people, blackmail and other meaninglessness, but the women were, as usual, perfect, with big breasts and swinging hips. As the film wore on I noticed that the scenes with the women in the skimpy lingerie seemed to upset my wife.

The film was about half over when I pushed the stop button and wrapped my arm around my wife's shoulders. "What's wrong, honey?" Her body was rigid and her jaw was set. "I'm sorry if something's upsetting you. Can I help?"

"It's nothing."

"It's not nothing, love. If you don't want to talk about it that's okay, but you're stiff as a board. You know I would never hurt you."

Her body softened a bit. "I know that. Let's just forget it."

She'd been fine before the film. "I'd like to help if I can. Was it something in the movie?" Since she didn't tell me to shut up, I continued. "It wasn't very different from lots of others we've seen, and those didn't seem to set you off. If watching them bothers you we'll never watch another one. I love you. Tell me and maybe I can fix it."

"You can't fix it. No one can."

I stayed silent hoping she'd continue. After a few moments she said, "I want to be beautiful."

Most people would not describe my wife as "pretty," but to me she has always been attractive. And I love her. She's a great wife, and a really sexy lady when she wants to be. What could I say that wouldn't be some empty cliché? I kept my mouth shut.

"I'm flat as a pancake and I hate my body." A tear trickled down her cheek. "I want to look like those women in the film. I want to have a hot, sexy body. I want you to look at me like you were looking at those models."

I hugged her close. "Oh, honey. Listen. I won't tell you that those women don't have great bodies. They should with all the tucking and lifting they've had. Most, if not all of them, are enhanced with gobs of silicone. They're picked for their shapes. No real people look like that, and neither do they without makeup and specially fitted clothes. You're here, in my arms, right where I want you. *You*, not them."

She smiled a weak little smile and snuggled against me. "I just want you to look at me the way you looked at them."

Later we cuddled in bed and slowly Bev relaxed. We didn't make love that night, but the following evening we were back to our old delicious tricks. I hadn't forgotten what she had said, however, and I wanted to do something to improve her feelings about herself. But how?

Throughout the following week I thought about the film and the lingerie that seemed to upset my wife. I considered what I could do to help and decided to take a big risk. What I was planning would either make things much better or much worse. I crossed my fingers and hoped for *better*. I knew her body and I wanted her exactly as she was. I just had to convince her of that.

On my lunch hour the following Friday afternoon I went to a local variety store and browsed through the undies. I was surprised at how much really nice stuff they had. I had checked my wife's bureau and discovered her size, so, on spec, I bought an inexpensive bright red bra and panty set, trimmed with black lace. As I walked toward the checkout, I thought about how my wife would look in the minuscule red nylon and almost drooled. To me she'd look as sexy as any of the women in the movie. I just hoped she'd feel the same way. I thought I'd be embarrassed when I checked out, but the bored sales associate ran the bar codes over the reader, took my credit card and shoved the red nylon into a plastic bag.

The following evening we went to a party with a few friends and were feeling pretty mellow by the time we got home. I sat on the edge of the bed and pulled Bev down beside me. *Be brave,* I told myself. *Take the risk. It could lead to a better attitude for her and all sorts of great sex for both of us.* "I bought you something yesterday." I hadn't gift wrapped it. Somehow that might make it seem important and I didn't want it to be a big deal, unless, of course, Bev saw it that way.

My wife looked puzzled. I'm not the spontaneous gift sort of guy. "What's the occasion, Don? It's not my birthday or anything."

"No occasion. Just a whim. Indulge me and open the bag." I felt all my muscles tighten, awaiting her reaction.

She opened the bag and pulled out the undies. She held them up and got a deer-in-the-headlights look. "Is this a joke?"

"Not at all. I know how you feel about your body, but I love you just the way you are. I hope these little items will convince you how much. I know I'd like to see you in them."

She looked horrified. "Me? You've got to be kidding."

"Of course you."

She looked suddenly frightened. "I don't think so." She pushed the bra and panties back into the bag.

I was not surprised at her quick dismissal, so I pressed on. "Why not?"

"That should be obvious." She became silent, but I waited. Finally she continued. "I don't look like those girls in the movie, the ones you ogled last weekend, and you can't convince me that I do."

"Of course you don't. I know what you look like, and I think you'd look really wonderful in these." I pulled the lingerie back out of the bag. "Please." I kissed the spot she particularly likes, the one just below her ear, then I nipped her earlobe. "Please," I whispered, my breath hot on her skin. "Just try them on for me."

BEV STARED AT THE TINY BITS OF NYLON AND LACE LYING SO innocently in her lap. She couldn't. She'd tried to gain weight, but it never seemed to happen. She'd never come even close to the voluptuous woman she wanted to be. As she looked up and saw the look on her husband's face, she wondered, *Can I take the risk? What if the sight of me turns him off?* He'd seen her naked almost every night of their married life, and the sight of her body hadn't turned him off yet.

Maybe the alcohol she'd had gave her an extra bit of courage. Without looking at Don, she scooped up the two pieces of red fabric and dashed into the bathroom. Before she could lose her nerve, she pulled off her jeans and shirt, then her underwear, and put on the lacy red bra and panties. They seemed to fit pretty well, but she didn't look down to check. The thong panties slipped between her cheeks, revealing, she knew, her skinny buttocks. But she loved her husband and he wanted this so much. She hesitated, then, without looking in the mirror, she opened the bathroom door and slowly walked back into the bedroom. Now she'd see the look of disappointment on his face. She almost pulled the undies off again, but she'd just give him what he wanted. Then he'd realize how dumb this idea had been.

As she walked from the bathroom, Bev was shocked at the look on Don's face. It was as if he'd never seen her before, and he seemed to like what he saw. She knew she didn't look like those lingerie models, but he was looking at her the same way he'd looked at them. His look of appreciation was enough reward to make the risk she'd taken well worth it. He looked almost stunned, with a heated gleam in his eyes. "Come here," he growled.

"But . . ."

He motioned her over, and she walked to the side of the bed, between his spread knees. "You look terrific," Don said. He flattened his hands and lightly rubbed the tips of the bra cups with his palms. Bev felt her nipples tighten and her knees weaken. "Terrific," he whispered again, sliding his hands around to the small of her back, then lower to cup her naked ass.

"I do?" Was he serious?

He pulled her to him and his mouth claimed one erect nipple through the nylon. She heard him make a low moaning sound deep in his throat. *I've never seen him get so hot so fast,* she thought, barely able to focus.

"You do, and not only do you look terrific, but you're here, for me, right now. That's what matters."

His hands seemed to be everywhere, and she had to brace her palms on his shoulders to prevent her knees from buckling. Heat flowed through her like warm honey, swelling her vaginal lips and soaking the crotch of her new panties.

When she reached behind her to unfasten the hooks of the bra, he pulled her hands away. "I like you just the way you are." He quickly pulled off his slacks and briefs, and she watched his cock spring free, proof of what he'd been saying. Even showing all her faults, she turned him on. He lay back on the bed and pulled her over onto him. His fingers found her crotch and he groaned, "You're wet. You want me."

She did. She wanted him very much.

He pulled the fabric aside and entered her, burying his hard cock deep inside. Without ever leaving her channel he pulled at her knees so she ended up crouched above him. Then he pushed her shoulders until she was sitting on his erection.

His large hands found her hips and raised her, then pushed her back down. She got the rhythm quickly and rocked up and down on his cock. She knew she was giving him pleasure, but she was less aroused until his thumb found her clit through the fabric and rubbed.

He'd never stroked her through material before and it felt different from their usual lovemaking. Muffled and sexy. The honey in her blood turned to molten lava and she felt her orgasm bubble up from low in her belly. As she felt spasms in her pussy, Don thrust harder and they came almost simultaneously.

Spasms subsiding, she fell onto him and realized that she was still wearing her new lingerie. "That was crazy," she said, panting, her pulse pounding.

"I know," Don said. "You looked so sexy."

Later, when they had calmed, they showered and climbed into bed. "What in the world happened?" Bev asked, still amazed.

"You happened, in that underwear. You looked sexy, but it's more than that. You looked ready to make love, eager to make love, and that's the most erotic thing there is."

She looked at her husband critically. He was balding and a little paunchy, but he was hers and she loved him. And she loved making love to him however he looked. Was that what he had been trying to tell her?

"I never knew anything like that lingerie would turn you on so. I watched you watching those women and I wanted to be one of them, to have you look at me like you look at them. Tonight you looked at me that way and it was fantastic."

"You looked like an invitation just for me. Maybe we can shop together next time."

"You bet," Bev said and curled against her husband. After twenty years of marriage there were still some surprises. How about that? How about that?

Getting Away from It All

※

THE WEATHER AT THE RESORT HAD BEEN PERFECT UP UNTIL that afternoon: azure skies with not a cloud, calm seas just right for sailing, a warm breeze that kept the Caribbean temperature at a precise eighty-five degrees and clear, starry nights made for intimacy. That's why Byron and I try to get a week there every couple of winters.

Well, that afternoon, at about four, the heavens opened and it poured. Big fat drops that quickly soaked everyone not under some kind of shelter. We asked the beautiful, chocolate-skinned bartender at the patio bar whether it would let up soon and she sadly shook her head. "We've had very little rain so far this year," she said in her wonderful lilting accent, "and we're glad to see it, but I'm sure you can do without. I'm really sorry, but it looks like the rest of the afternoon's going to be a washout."

I sipped my Caribbean Queen, a combination of several colorful liquors and fruit juices, and looked at Byron. "What should we do for the rest of the afternoon?"

He caught my eye and said, "I'm sure I can think of something." I was immediately thinking what he was thinking. We'd been making love almost every evening since we got here. It's amazing what taking the pressures of everyday life off one's shoulders does for the libido.

The bartender interrupted our delicious train of thought. "We'll have indoor games and stuff in the Mirage Room. I'm sure you'll have lots of fun."

Byron winked at me. "I'm sure we will." He grabbed his drink from the table, took my hand and said, "How about we go back to the room?"

I grabbed my drink and followed him. I loved that gleam in his eye and I didn't want to pass up this opportunity.

Back in our room Byron suggested that, since we were both covered in sunscreen, we should take a shower. Together. That sounded good to me, so we stripped and Byron adjusted the water temperature. We climbed beneath the soft spray and took several minutes to scrub off the oil. Then he teased, "I'm not sure you got all the places that needed washing." He lathered his hand and started on my back. "I wouldn't want you to miss a spot."

I giggled and said, "Of course not." Needless to say, I love the feel of Byron's hands on my skin. He slid his slick fingers over my spine, down to my ass. Then his fingers slipped into my crack. We'd never tried anal sex. Byron had suggested it, sort of kiddingly, a few months back, but I had steered the conversation in another direction. I didn't know then whether I wanted to try backdoor play, but I had to admit that the feeling of his hands pulling my cheeks apart and his one finger lightly touching my hole was very erotic. Maybe.

Knowing my previous reluctance, he backed off. "Just trying to get all of you clean," he said. "Now turn around."

His soapy hands massaged my breasts, pulling at the nipples until they stood out in hard points. When he started to slip down to my pussy I pulled back. "Not so fast, buster," I said, slapping his hands away. "My turn."

"Of course," he said, turning. I soaped my hands and rubbed his back as he had mine. God, I love the feel of his hard muscles beneath my hands. My fingers slithered over his skin and down to his ass. I knew how hot his hands had made me, so I cupped his cheeks in my palms and squeezed, rubbing his cheeks against each other. I heard his breath catch. Hmm. He was as aroused as I was by the thought of rear play. Hmm.

I took hold of his shoulders and turned him until he faced me. His cock was rigid. Byron has thick chest hair and I love to run my fingers through it, so I soaped my hands and combed through his mat, finding his nipples and scratching them lightly with my nails. I had never thought a man's nipples would be as sensitive as a woman's, but Byron proved me wrong. I felt them tighten and become as erect as mine. "You're making me crazy, love," he growled.

"I hope so. It would be a shame if only one of us was turned on."

This resort had French-style shower heads, the kind that are attached by a hose. Byron lifted the head from the bracket and sprayed my chest. Then he leaned over and licked the water off the tips of my breasts. Over and over he sprayed my skin, then licked it off with his rough tongue. He held me close and whispered in my ear, "I've been thinking about something for a long time, but I don't want to turn you off."

Byron and I have been together for four years, and I knew from the sound of his voice that he'd suddenly gotten serious. I stayed silent, letting him continue at his own pace. "I want you to understand that you're never to do anything *just* to please me. You understand that, right?"

"Of course." I decided to help the conversation along. "I think I know what you're suggesting, but I'm not really sure how I feel about anal sex."

"It's something I've always wanted to try," Byron said, "but I've never been with any woman I'd trust to say stop if things got too heavy. I don't want this to be anything but pleasurable for both of us."

"I don't know whether I'd like it, but I do trust you completely. I know you'd stop if I asked you to, so that makes many things possible."

"Possible? It's okay?"

"It's okay so far."

His face lit up. "Okay. I've done some reading and anal sex doesn't have to include penetration. Why don't we see what turns you on?" He moved behind me, held the sprayer against my back, and water cascaded down my spine. He slid one finger between my cheeks and touched my anus. "Does this feel good or not?"

"I have to admit," I said, feeling my pussy swell, "it feels pretty hot."

"Honest?"

"Honest. I promise to stop you if I want to."

He pulled his finger back. "I'm going to make it soapy."

I felt his fingers slide around my hole. I had always considered anal play dirty and nasty, but in the shower, all squeaky clean, it felt really good. My pussy twitched and I ached to touch myself and ease my needs. I didn't. I let the tension build.

Suddenly he pushed, just a bit, and the tip of his slippery, soapy finger penetrated. It was incredibly erotic and I reflexively pushed against him so the digit slipped in more deeply. Byron reached around and massaged my slit, moving his finger on my clit in the rhythm of his finger in my ass. Suddenly, with little warning, I came, hard. "Oh God," I cried, unable to catch my breath. "Oh God." Spasms rocked through me, causing my knees to buckle. Byron held me up, supporting me until I was able to stand again. "Shit, baby," he said. "That was so fast."

"Caught me unawares," I said, breathless. "I never imagined."

"Neither did I." He put the shower head back into its bracket but left the spray on.

I knew he was still fully aroused, so I knelt beneath the cascading water and took his cock in my mouth. I used every trick I knew to give him as much pleasure as he'd given me. I swirled my tongue around the head, then sucked the length of him into my mouth. I created a slight vacuum and felt his cock twitch. I decided to try a little anal stimulation on him, so I soaped my hands, cupped his balls, then slid one finger into his ass crack and rimmed his asshole. He must have liked it as much as I had, since he quickly filled my mouth with his semen, groaning. Amazingly I felt the spasms of his cock in the muscles around the edge of his asshole.

I swallowed quickly, then we sort of helped each other out of the shower, turning off the water and wrapping each other in the thick towels the resort had provided. We fell onto the bed and dozed.

Later Byron said, "I'm shocked and delighted by what happened earlier."

"Me too," I readily admitted. "I've been reluctant to try that kind of stuff, but I guess we've been missing something really good. I don't know whether I want to take this any further, but this afternoon was a wonderful first step."

"We'll take it a little at a time."

"I'm willing," I said, "and I'll always associate the sound of rain on the roof with what happened today." A clap of thunder echoed through the room. I wondered how long the storm had been raging. Byron hugged me, knowing of my instinctive fear of nature's pyrotechnics. "Great sex is great therapy. Thunderstorms will never feel quite as scary again."

An Arrogant Ass Gets His

❧

I GUESS I'VE BEEN A SUN WORSHIPER SINCE I WAS A LITTLE girl. I remember spending every one of my school vacations at the beach with my parents, soaking up rays. I'm quite dark skinned to begin with so I never burned. Rather, my skin tone would deepen until I was the color of fine cognac.

Now that I'm an adult, I'm much more careful. I've learned how harmful sun can be to the skin, but I still love the feeling of the hot rays on my skin. So I slather myself with number forty-five sunscreen and, whenever I can, I bask. Last weekend, my best friends, Arty and Jane Matthews, left the care of their luxurious redwood, aboveground pool to me, so on Saturday, once I had finished testing the water and adding chemicals, I changed into my briefest bikini, covered myself with sunscreen and stretched out on the deck in one of their most comfortable lounge chairs, put my iPod earphones in my ears and baked.

I must have dozed, but I was startled awake by the loud scraping sound of a chair being moved across the deck. I guess I made a noise because as I looked at the young man who was turning to sit down, he appeared to be as surprised as I was. "Who are you?" I asked, pulling the iPod from my ears.

"I was about to ask you the same question," he snapped. "My name's Vince Chiccone and I'm the Matthews' next door neighbor. And you?"

"I'm Brynn Patterson and I'm Jane's best friend. She asked me to check the pool chemicals each weekend while they're away." I looked him over. He appeared to be in his twenties, as I was, with a body that said he worked out. I'm a sucker for gorgeous abs and he had them. His every move was obviously calculated to show off his muscles, and his brief Speedos hid nothing of his other accoutrements. *This might liven up an otherwise dull afternoon,* I thought.

"She asked me to do the same thing," he said, his face softening. "Insisted, actually." He paused, then said, "Oh, shit, you're *that* Brynn."

"How many Brynns do you know? And what do you mean, *that* Brynn?"

Vince chuckled. "Jane has been after me to meet her best friend, Brynn, for months now. I absolutely hate blind anythings, and I told her so in no uncertain terms. She must have set this up." His gaze now traveled slowly over my near-naked body. "I must admit, I'm sorry now I didn't take her up on her offer ages ago. We could be making beautiful music together by now."

"You can turn off the charm, lover boy. I'm not impressed." He was undoubtedly beautiful, but sadly, the minute he'd opened his mouth, he'd ruined it all. I was really surprised at Jane, who usually had better taste. I sighed. Too bad. He might have been fun.

"Well, *I* am impressed by *you*." There was almost a leer in his voice. "God, you've got a body that won't quit. Come on, sexy, let's play."

He reached for my hand, but with a slight harrumph, I turned over onto my belly away from Vince's gaze. I heard him chuckle and found heat flowing through me that had nothing to do with the sun. I have to admit that there was something magnetic, almost overpowering, about him, but he was coming on much too strongly for me. Although I'm a free spirit and enjoy an adventurous quickie from time to time, I like to do my own choosing, or at least cooperate in the mating rituals. I don't like being picked up, especially by someone quite so cocksure. I hated his arrogance, and I wanted nothing more than to show him a thing or two. I snorted. I had no real intentions in any direction, but if something came up, well . . .

"Okay. I get it," he said to my back. "You like to control your relationships with men. You're one of those 'liberated women.'" He said it with what was almost a snarl.

sLord, save me. I sighed, my back still toward him. "I don't like being picked up by audacious men who have more nerve than brains."

"Okay, sweetheart, your loss. It could have been really great."

I snorted, put my earphones back in my ears and tried to tune him out. *He's just too much,* I thought. *What an arrogant ass. He deserves whatever he gets. And more.* The idea of having sex with this gorgeous hunk did turn me on, but it would have to be my way.

As I lay there, I began to think about the contents of the Matthews' garage and of a way to have some fun. Putting my iPod into my carry-all, I slowly got up, slipped on my light coverup and made quite a production of checking the pool chemicals again while he watched my body through the lacy fabric. I sexed up my walk and wiggled my hips, and while bending over to scoop water from the pool, I let him get a good look at the narrow crotch of my bikini bottom.

Although the pool chemicals were perfect, I bustled around as if I had to add something to the crystal water. I slipped on my flip-flops and climbed down the ladder, knowing Vince's eyes did not leave my body until I was out of sight. I heard him settle back on his chair and turn on the poolside CD player to some New Age nonsense. In the garage, I waited until I thought he would be relaxed, then picked up a bucket of chlorine tablets, put a large roll of duct tape and a pair of scissors on top and quietly climbed back onto the deck.

Putting down the bucket, I walked slowly behind Vince's chair and saw that, as I had hoped, he was almost asleep, his arms relaxed on the armrests of the lounge. Quietly and carefully I unrolled a length of tape and, with just a few quick twists, wrapped several lengths around his forearms, fastening them to the chair. Before he could fully comprehend what was going on, I had his lower legs firmly attached to the bottom of the chair as well.

"Now, you arrogant idiot," I said, standing so I was backlit by the bright sun, "here's the way things are."

The chair bounced as he struggled but could get nowhere with his bonds. "You must be some kind of a nut. Listen, lady. I don't know what you're doing, but I suggest that you unwrap this stuff before I call the cops."

"I have no intention of 'unwrapping this stuff,' as you put it, so forget it, and I'm not sure how you're planning to call anyone. I would suggest that you be nice or I'll just leave you here."

He continued to wiggle, making the chair creep across the deck, while loudly protesting his treatment.

"I would be careful if I were you," I said sweetly. "Too much bouncing and you'll end up in the pool. Do you think you can swim with a chair taped to your body?"

He calmed and closed his mouth. "Good," I said. "You're getting the picture."

He silently glared at me.

I crossed my arms and tapped my foot. "When you first saw me you wanted to have some fun, and I think that's a great idea."

"Well, all right," he said, suddenly perking up.

"However, we'll have it my way. You will do what I say, when I say it. Do you understand?"

It was obvious that he wasn't used to being on the receiving end of macho moves, but he was slowly grasping the fact that he really didn't have any choice. With an exasperated breath, he said, "Okay. I get it."

"Good. First, let's get a look at what you're offering." I took the scissors and cut up the sides of his Speedos and pulled them off. He did have a great cock, large, hard and twitching. I cupped his balls and squeezed lightly. "Nice package. We'll put it to use. Eventually."

"Eventually? I'm ready now, sugar."

"Cut the crap. This is now my party and I'll play the way I want to. And don't call me *sugar*." I scooped a bucket of water from the pool and poured it onto his groin. "Just to cool you off a bit." I don't think it did the job since his throbbing dick was still hard as stone. "Oh, well," I said, staring at his crotch, "I guess that didn't work. You'll just have to be patient all on your own."

I pulled a chair close to his, head to foot, and lay on it until he had a good view of my crotch. Then I wiggled out of my top, cupped my breasts and pulled at my nipples. "I think I have nice breasts. Don't you?"

"Yes," he said, his voice almost a growl. I could see his fingers twitching, trying to get at my tits. "Naughty," I said, slapping playfully at his bound wrists. "Can't touch."

I spent a long time playing with my tits. I love doing it, and I pinch my nipples hard while I masturbate. I felt my pussy react and knew my juices were flowing.

"Listen, sweetheart," he whined. "You're obviously having your fun, but this is ridiculous. You're making me crazy and you're making yourself hot too. You need me and I just want to help you get off."

I raised one eyebrow. "Help me? I don't need your help. Women enjoy making love with a guy sometimes, but we're also quite capable of satisfying our own needs. As you'll see."

"But, baby . . ."

"I'm not your baby." I pulled off the bottom of my suit and let him have a good look at my swollen pussy. "I love the aroma of sex. Can you smell how hot I am?"

He took a deep breath. "God, yes," he said, cock waving in the air.

"Good." I rubbed my clit in just the right way and felt my first climax building in my belly. "If I rub . . . right . . . here," I said, "I'll come." I moaned as orgasm crashed over me. It was extraexotic knowing he was watching my every move.

"Shit, baby, I wanted to be inside of you when you came," he whined.

"You might be next time," I said, calming. My first orgasms are always quick and hard. "Let's see how many times I can come."

His whining grew more insistent. "I want to fuck you."

"Fucking's not everything. Even a quickie should be like making love. I don't fuck myself; I make love to my body."

With Vince staring at my fingers I rubbed again, and as I'd known I could, I came for a second time. I allowed myself the luxury of slowly calming, then minutes later I said, "Now I have time for a little fun." I untaped one of Vince's arms and guided his hand to my pussy. "Can you bring me off again? It's not too difficult. Even you should be able to accomplish that."

His fingers found my slit and fumbled around. "Hey, slow down." I guided his fingers and showed him how I liked it. Sure enough, I came a third time.

"Mmm," I purred. "That was quite good. There might be hope for you after all."

He smiled, not the arrogant ass smile he'd had before, but genuine pleasure showed on his face. He was learning. "I'm glad I pleased you."

"Now," I said trying to look puzzled, "what should we do?"

"I still want to fuck you," he said softly, genuine regret in his voice. He paused, then said, "I mean, I want to make love to you."

I didn't know how sincere he was, but I was willing to give him the benefit of the doubt. And I wanted him. I looked at his cock sticking straight up from his crotch. "Maybe you do. Will you be nice?"

His grin was soft and easy, and there was remorse in his eyes. "I'm really sorry about before. You were right. I was an arrogant ass. I really would like to make love to you."

"Make love *with* me. That's what this is all about." I found a condom in my purse and unrolled it over his erection. "Ready?"

He laughed, and I joined him. I straddled the chair, lowered my pussy onto his cock, then held completely still. Then I unfastened his other wrist and guided his hands to my breasts. He played, massaging my flesh and pulling at my nipples the way I had. He guided my upper body toward his mouth and suckled, flicking his tongue over my nubs. All the while his cock was deep inside of me but his hips were still. "You're being very patient," I said.

"I'm trying, but I'm also very, very horny. Are you ready for me to fuck you?"

"For *me* to make love with *you*, you mean."

He smiled at me. "Yeah, that's exactly what I mean."

I levered myself so I rose and fell on his cock, but I wasn't able to get the right rhythm. "I can help, if you want," he said, sensing my frustration. "Untie my legs."

I got up and unfastened the tape around his ankles. Then he

lowered the back of the chair, turned us both over and stretched out on top of me. With one swift motion he was inside me, thrusting, using the entire length of his cock to please us both. He pulled out, used the tip of his penis to rub my clit, and then he was inside me again. Even though I knew he needed to come, he played with me, driving me higher until, with one long thrust I came, a long low moan echoing deep in my chest.

Only then did he let himself come with a growl. He'd waited. Maybe there was something worthwhile beneath his arrogance.

Later, lying side by side on lounge chairs, we soaked the sun in silence. "I don't know what to say," he said finally.

"Neither do I. I've never done anything like that before."

"It's out of my league too, but as I think over what happened, I'm afraid I deserved it."

I looked at him and smiled. "You did."

"And I'm sorry. Can we start all over?"

"Nope. I like it just as it is."

"Does that mean we can get together one evening for dinner?"

I pretended to think about it, then I said, "Are you busy later this evening?"

His grin was his answer. Will this relationship go anywhere? Who knows? Can I reform an arrogant ass? Do I want to? I'll have to think about that.

Mr. Fix-It

$\approx$

My husband is a regular Mr. Fix-It, and it saves us quite a bit of money each year. He does all kinds of minor electrical work around our house and he paints up a storm, sometimes with me helping. He regrouts the bathroom tiles, installs new light fixtures and does basic plumbing, keeping our three-bedroom condo in the suburbs shipshape.

One evening, when the kids were away at summer camp, our central air-conditioning system went kablooey. It started making some kind of weird noise, and a little water leaked out from the enclosure where the main part is. Troy, alias Mr. Fix-It, went to work in the tiny space where the stuff is housed. Let me explain that our AC unit has two parts, one outside on the patio and one in a closetlike room that's almost inaccessible because of the wall unit that's pushed close to the door. "I think it's something in the condenser," he said, banging around in the tight space. He'd wriggled in, and now he wriggled out and dusted his hands off.

Ahh, the condenser. So that's what this inside part is called. Or maybe it's the outside part. Whatever. As long as Troy knows. "Honey," he said, "I need you to hold something here while I check outside."

He had wrapped a rag around a leaking hose and showed me where to hold it while he looked at the outside part. I wriggled into the confined space, my ass sticking into the living room, and grabbed the rag where he'd shown me. Already a small amount of water had run down the hose. "How about getting a bucket so the water won't soak the rug?" I called as he scurried out the door.

"Not necessary. I'll just be a moment. Don't let go."

So I held the rag around the hose and heard him outside. "Just another minute," he yelled.

Great. There I was, stuck in an awkward position with my ass in the air and both hands wrapped around a drippy rag. "Make it snappy," I said. "My legs are all cramped."

I heard him come back inside, then stop. "That's quite a position you're in," he said, his voice suddenly soft.

"It is, and it's damned uncomfortable." I tried to turn and look at him, but I couldn't move without letting go and risking dirty water soaking into my new beige carpeting.

"Yeah," he said, "and your butt looks great too." I could hear him chuckle.

"Fuck the smart-ass comments," I said, resorting to the kind of language I rarely use. "Just get me out of here."

"Smart-ass. I get it," he said, latching on to my unintended pun.

"Don't be a wise guy. Just get me out of here." I was repeating myself but one leg was starting to hurt.

"Not so fast," Troy said. "I kind of like looking at you."

"My arms are getting tired and my legs are cramped," I whined. "Just fix this thing so I can get up."

I heard him behind me, then I felt his hand on my ass, stroking and fondling, his fingers tickling my crotch. I couldn't help but laugh. "Okay, lover boy, stop messing around and fix this thing."

"And spoil my fun?"

His fingers rubbed my crotch more insistently, and to my chagrin I found myself getting excited. I wanted to berate him, but his hand felt really good.

"I'm suddenly not in any hurry," he said, and I heard him walk into the kitchen and return. "Let's see what I can do to make you more comfortable." I heard the snick of scissors and quickly Troy had cut up the back of my tee shirt, then across the sleeves. It pulled off in his hand. "Don't let go, now," he said as I started to move, "or the carpet will be ruined."

"Cut it out," I said, torn between arousal, good humor and mild annoyance.

"Not on your life. This is too good to waste."

Since I wasn't wearing a bra I was now naked from the waist up, and Troy made good use of that fact. He cupped my large breasts from behind and began to play with my nipples. He knows that my nipples are my weak spot, and as he pulled and pinched I found myself moistening despite my uncomfortable position.

Then his mouth found my shoulder and he kissed and nibbled the back of my neck, hands still kneading my breasts. I was getting really hot, but I couldn't move to touch him without letting go. I was stuck with my hands on the hose. I wished it were his cock, but . . .

I felt the scissors on the waistband of my shorts. "I'll buy you new ones," Troy said as he cut them and my panties off. Then his hands were in my sopping crotch, feeling, delving, playing, driving me ever higher. I could barely breathe and my knees were shaking despite my unusual position. "You know, I've always wanted to play this way," he said. "Hang on."

He left then. Hang on? What choice did I have? The rag was soaked and a tiny trickle of water was dribbling down my arm toward my elbow. At the same time my own fluids trickled down my thighs.

I heard Troy return and I tried to turn to see where he'd been, but my head was buried in the closet, trapped beside the AC. "I brought some fun," he said, and I felt cold plastic rubbing against the heated flesh between my legs. He'd been in the toy box.

Slowly he filled my pussy with a thick dildo, and I thought I'd come right then. I guess what kept me from the peak of excitement was the discomfort of my position. Was that the bad news or the good?

Then another dildo slid over my flowing juices and found my rear hole. He pushed it inside and lodged it firmly in my ass. He proceeded to play with the two of them, sliding first one, then the other, in and out of my openings. I thought I'd died and gone to arousal heaven. He was driving me absolutely crazy.

"My turn," he said, pulling the dildo from my pussy and rubbing my slit with the tip of his cock. He pulled my knees back a little so my crotch was more accessible to him. He crouched behind me and, amazingly enough, managed to slide his cock into my pussy. Then he was pounding inside me, every thrust rubbing against the dildo still lodged in my ass. I couldn't hold back any longer and I came, rockets going off, waves of hot lava filling my entire body. I heard the characteristic moan of Troy's climax as I started to come down.

He tumbled me back so we were both lying on the rug. "Holy shit," he said. "I couldn't resist."

We were on the carpet and my hands were no longer around the rag. I looked at the hose expecting to see water flowing out, but saw it was dry. "Okay, buster," I said, playfully cuffing him on the shoulder. "What's with the hose?"

"Oh, I found the problem in the drainpipe. Dirt had clogged the outlet. When I cleared it, all the water flowed out."

I was incensed. "You mean all the time I thought I was trapped in that closet the problem was already fixed?"

He rubbed my pussy, still sopping with my juices and his. "Got a problem with that?"

I wanted to be angry, but the sex had been the best in a long time. I let out a long sigh. "I want to be mad," I said. Then I laughed.

"I know. Forgive me?"

"I forgive you." But I'll get even one day.

Surfing

❦

"WHAT'S WITH THE GRIN?" CAROLYN ASKED AS SHE SETTLED onto a park bench beside the play area and watched her three-year-old, Rachel, scamper off toward the sandbox.

"What grin?" Carolyn's friend Joanne answered, her eyes never leaving her two-and-a-half-year-old son. The two women had known each other for several months, ever since they had started meeting several afternoons a week on the same bench with their kids. Carolyn worked only two days a week and Joanne was a stay-at-home mom, so they'd spent quite a few afternoons together. The two couples had gone to the movies together a few times too, when they could get sitters.

Carolyn laughed. "That grin on your face that says, 'I got mine last night.'"

With a giggle, Joanne said, "Oh, *that* grin. Yeah, Ian and I have a great time in the bedroom. And it wasn't just last night; it was this morning before he went to work too."

"Well, well, well," Carolyn said, eyebrows waggling Groucho Marx style. "You guys sure seem to have a very active sex life."

"It's great as long as my darling son, Greg, keeps sleeping late."

Carolyn sighed and leaned back on the bench. Ian was of average height and not too good-looking. She'd never really thought of him as a sex partner before, but from Joanne's attitude, Carolyn thought he must be pretty special. "God, you're so lucky. I can't remember when Gerry and I last had that shit-eating-grin kind of great sex."

Joanne shifted and recrossed her legs, seeming a little embarrassed. "Yeah, until recently we weren't either." Her grin widened. "Now it's so fabulous."

"What changed things?"

"I guess I can talk frankly with you."

"Of course you can." Carolyn leaned toward her. "Give, girl."

"Well, we got a new toy. It arrived yesterday, and Ian just couldn't wait to try it out."

"Toy? What kind of toy?"

"This is really embarrassing," Joanne said, coloring slightly. She leaned forward and her voice dropped. "We've been shopping on the Internet and a wonderful little package he ordered finally came."

Carolyn was horrified. "You shopped on the Net? You ordered from one of those sleazy companies? Aren't you worried that you'll be scammed? And don't you get on some of those weird mailing lists and stuff?"

Joanne looked at Carolyn seriously. "All the sites on the Net aren't sleazy. As a matter of fact most of them represent serious companies. I'm sure there are a few clunkers, but this is a really big, reputable one with stores in California too."

"You're kidding."

"Not in the least. Actually Ian and I have ordered from a few sites." She mentioned the names of three. "We've never had a problem. Sure, we get on a few outlandish mailing lists, but we use an alternate screen name so even that's not a problem. And I have to tell you, just looking through this particular website led to several great nights, even before we ordered anything. You sound like someone who might be interested."

"I'm listening carefully," Carolyn said with a tilt of her head. "Does the stuff really arrive in a plain brown wrapper?"

"It certainly does. No one knows what's in the ordinary little box. Or yesterday's big one for that matter." She giggled.

"What did you buy?"

"I'm not sure Ian would want me to share that little bit of information. Let's just say that we had sex in a whole new way." At that moment Greg crammed a handful of sand into his mouth and Joanne ran over to dislodge it. Disappointed, Carolyn sensed that the topic wouldn't be brought up again that day, and it wasn't.

Later that afternoon, while Rachel was taking a late-afternoon nap, Carolyn booted up her computer and, after some initial hesitation, brought up a search engine and looked up one of the companies Joanne had mentioned. When the hyperlink came up, she clicked on it and arrived at a site that completely surprised her. The atmosphere was soft and easy, with no pictures of naked women or pop-up ads. For almost fifteen minutes she clicked around the site, then closed the window and, with a long sigh, signed off.

That evening after dinner, as she and Gerry sat at the dinner table while Rachel played with a cookie in her high chair, Carolyn said, "I sat with Joanne this afternoon. She and Ian really seem to have quite a sex life."

Gerry laughed. "I know. I see him on the subway from time to time and he won't let me forget how hot his wife is."

Carolyn had never thought of Joanne as hot before. "Do *you* think she's sexy?"

"Sure. She's pretty and she's got a great body. But she's not as hot as you, baby."

"Thanks for that." Her smile softened her words. She wasn't really jealous. She liked Joanne and didn't mind if Gerry found Joanne attractive as long as that was all he did. "Anyway, Joanne told me that she and Ian have done some shopping online."

"I gather you can get some pretty good prices on electronics and stuff, even when you have to pay for shipping."

Carolyn shifted her position. She had been intrigued and turned on by some of the merchandise she'd seen on the website and hoped Gerry would be curious too. "Actually, it's not electronics she was talking about."

She watched Gerry's attention focus on her. "Oh? So what type of stuff were you talking about?"

Carolyn swallowed hard. Nothing ventured . . . "Toys. Sexy stuff. I looked at a few of the sites Joanne mentioned this afternoon. It's really amazing what those places sell."

Gerry's eyebrows shot up toward his hairline. "Really?"

Carolyn had risked enough and wasn't sure how the website information had gone over, so she turned to Rachel and lifted her from her high chair. "Okay, sweets, time for your bath."

After Rachel's bath, Gerry came in to the baby's room and helped put her to bed. While Gerry read a story to his daughter, Carolyn tidied the kitchen, wondering whether the subject of sex toys would ever come up again. *Probably not,* she thought. *Gerry's not the adventurous type.*

A half hour later, when Carolyn wandered into the bedroom, she found Gerry sitting at the computer. "I found the link you used this afternoon," he said, "and clicked over. Interesting site."

Carolyn's entire body tensed. Was he going to tease her about this? She studied him, and judging her husband's body language, she thought he might be intrigued by what he was looking at. The whole thing made Carolyn a little uncomfortable, but there was something illicit and delicious there too. "Did you find anything special?" she asked tentatively.

Without looking up from the screen, he patted his thigh. "Come sit here and let's look around."

Gerry hadn't invited her to sit on his lap in ages, so Carolyn settled down gently and looked at the screen. Filling the frame was a picture of an oddly shaped vibrator. "Ever owned one of these?" he asked. "I mean, like before we were married?"

"No," she said. "I never owned anything like that."

Without hesitation, he said, "Okay, let's get one." He clicked, typed and soon he had not only ordered the vibrator but he'd also created a user name and password so he could return to the site and order more. While her husband typed, Carolyn could feel his penis swelling and she realized that she was also getting very excited.

It took only moments for Gerry to finish on the site, shut down the computer and drag his wife into bed. "The whole thing makes me hungry for you," he said hoarsely. His mouth found hers and his tongue plundered. His hands kneaded her breasts and squeezed her the way she liked. "Take all those clothes off."

As she undressed, with the small part of her brain that still worked through the erotic haze, she thought, *This is fabulous. Gerry's hasn't been this hot in a very long time. It's amazing what a little shopping can do.* Naked, she lay on the bed and quickly Gerry was beside her. She tangled her fingers in his hair and pulled his head to her nipple. He suckled, pulling a little more roughly than he usually did, quickly driving her toward orgasm. Then his fingers found her wet core and drove into her, first two, then three, filling her totally.

She cupped his buttocks as he finger fucked her, then she

wrapped her hand around his hard cock and squeezed. It was happening really quickly, but she wanted it even faster. She put her hands on her husband's waist and guided his erection to her sopping pussy. They were both so hot that he was quickly inside her, pounding and bellowing. It only took a moment for her to catch up with him, and they came almost simultaneously.

"Holy shit," Gerry said. "That shopping we just did made me really horny."

"Me too," Carolyn said, catching her breath.

"I can't wait until the package arrives."

Me neither, Carolyn thought. *Thanks, Joanne.*

Surfing: The Aftermath

❧

THE PARCEL ARRIVED IN THE MAILBOX ABOUT FOUR DAYS later. At first Carolyn didn't realize what the simple brown box was, then she remembered and her pussy twitched. That evening of great sex with Gerry had been repeated the following evening. Was it only a coincidence? She didn't think so.

She put the box in her bedside table drawer, then took Rachel to the supermarket. All afternoon, however, her mind kept straying to the package. She'd never owned a sex toy, even though several of her school friends bragged about their collections of dildos, vibrators and nipple clamps. She'd always thought most of it was just talk, but now she wasn't so sure. Certainly her friend Joanne hadn't been shy to admit that she and her husband had quite a toy collection.

Gerry got home at his usual time. They had dinner as they always did, spending time feeding Rachel, and then, while Carolyn did the dishes, Gerry put their daughter to bed and read her a story. Carolyn wanted to mention the little box but she kept quiet.

Did she really want to do this? It was deeply embarrassing, but deliciously so, so she kept it to herself until she had kissed Rachel good night and wandered into the bedroom to watch TV with her husband. "That box arrived today," she said quietly.

"Box?" Getty said, looking blank. Then she watched as comprehension dawned. "Oh, *that* box." He looked at her quizzically. "Did you open it?"

"No, of course not."

Gerry turned and took Carolyn in his arms. "Did you wonder about it?" He nibbled on her neck.

"I guess I did a little," she admitted, tilting her head so he could get a better angle.

"I've thought a lot about what we've done recently and I like it a lot," he said. "Carl even commented a couple of times on my shit-eating grin when I saw him at the subway station. Good sex will do that to a guy." His smile widened. "Great sex will do it even more."

"It's been good—well, great really, hasn't it?"

"You bet. Shall we see what's in the package?"

Thinking about their recent nights and about what was in the box had Carolyn's vaginal tissues swollen and slippery, and all she could think about was having Gerry inside of her. "Sure," she said quickly.

"Impatient?" Gerry asked, sensing her mood as he usually could.

She shyly lowered her chin. "Yes," she said. "Very."

"Me too. But I'm also curious and eager to unwrap our little goodie."

Carolyn retrieved the brown box from her bedside table and handed it to her husband, settling beside him on the bed. She realized that her hands were shaking. "You do it."

With little preamble Gerry tore open the box and ripped open the plastic that housed the vibrator. "I read on the site that it came with batteries."

Carolyn swallowed hard, unable to speak. The thing was almost mesmerizing. Long and thick, the flesh-colored vibrator had a small projection at the base. A "clitoral stimulator," the web page description had said. She'd read articles and stories about vibrators, but she'd never seen one up close before.

Gerry fussed and finally got the remaining plastic packaging off, then inserted the batteries in the base. "Okay, let's see how this puppy works." He pressed the control housed at the end of a long plastic wire and the toy made a light humming sound. "Take off your clothes and let's try it out."

No foreplay? Well, Carolyn thought, *I'm so hot I don't really need any.* She peeled off her shirt and jeans, and was about to remove her bra and panties when Gerry said, "No, leave those on." He stripped to his shorts, which left no doubt that he was fully aroused. "Lie down here," he said, patting the bed.

Carolyn stretched out and Gerry touched her hot, wet vaginal lips through her panties with the cool plastic. "Here's what it feels like when it's turned on." He pushed the slider and the toy hummed.

"It tickles," Carolyn squeaked.

"It's supposed to, sort of." He moved the buzzing tip to one nipple. Through the fabric of her bra, Carolyn could feel the vibrations, making her bud tighten. "Umm, your tit likes this," Gerry said. He shifted to the other breast and her other nipple became tightly erect. "Your body is very responsive. How about here?"

He pressed it against her belly and she squirmed away. "That tickles and it's not really good."

"Okay, we'll make an inventory. Nipples yes, belly no. How about here?" He stroked Carolyn's inner thigh. "Good or bad?"

"Pretty good," she said, "but it makes me even more hungry."

Ignoring her hint, he touched higher on her thigh. "How about here?" he said, moving the vibrating tip down her leg. "Good or bad?"

"Good," she admitted, "but frustrating."

"I'll bet it makes you hungry for this." He parted her thighs farther, and when he touched the center of her body through her panties, she jumped.

"Good," she said, her heart suddenly pounding and her body actually shaking. "Oh, baby, very good."

"Let's see," he said, leering. "Better here," he said, sliding the toy toward her opening, "or here?" He touched the tip of her clit.

"Right there," she said, climbing, almost climaxing from that alone.

"Can I make you come just from this?"

"Yes." She was almost incoherent with lust.

"Then this should be even better." He turned off the buzzing, pulled the edge of her panties aside and pushed the now-quiet toy inside. Then he pulled the fabric back over the phallus and stood up, control in his hand. "We need more testing."

He pushed the slider that controlled the vibrations to about half speed. The humming inside her body was making Carolyn's belly clench; she tightened her vaginal muscles to better feel it. She arched her back, wanting, needing.

"Better like this," Gerry said, "or like this?" He pushed the slider up to maximum and the buzz increased. Then he pushed another button and the clitoral stimulator, already pressed against her flesh, began to vibrate.

She felt the jolt throughout her body. "If you leave that this way," she panted, "I'm going to come."

"I can deal with that."

So she let go, her vaginal muscles clamping rhythmically around the slender wand. "Yes, baby, like that," she yelled.

Gerry left the toy inside as he stripped off his shorts. Then he pulled it out and replaced it with his hard cock. He thrust into her with long, hard strokes, and when he came, Carolyn came for the second time. She was amazed. She'd never climaxed twice in a row before.

Several minutes passed before either of them could speak. Finally, Gerry said, "That was amazing. Did you actually climax twice? It sure felt like you did."

"I certainly did. It's never happened to me like that before. I was so hot, I just exploded."

"Me too. That toy is dynamite."

Carolyn picked it up, still humming. She touched it to her husband's now-flaccid cock. "Next time I want to see how you like it. We'll need lots of testing."

"Then we'll have to go back to the website and explore some more. I'm sure we can find other little goodies to buy."

"You bet."

A Sexual Adventure

✦

I HAVE A FANTASY. I WOULDN'T EVER DREAM OF BEHAVING AS I do in my dream, of course, but I'm not reticent in my mind. Let me tell you about it.

The fantasy began when my friend Darleen told me about something called "A Sexual Adventure." She's a really free spirit and loves to find bizarre erotic exploits. It's totally safe, she told me, and went on to explain that several of her friends had done it and raved. She wouldn't tell me any of the actual details, just giggled and said it would be like nothing I'd ever done before and that I'd really love it.

Since I've always been a sexual experimenter, and I'm usually up for anything, I agreed.

In my fantasy I have no idea exactly where I am or how I came to be here. *What have I gotten myself into?* I wonder. I am blindfolded and naked and I've never felt this helpless before. It's really erotic but a little scary too. I sigh and wiggle my fingers and toes to remind me they're still part of my body as I focus on my surroundings and try to figure out what's going on. I can hear the din of dozens of voices in the background and what might be the clink of glasses and plates. Could I be in some kind of restaurant, club or theater? I can smell food or the remains of it. Suddenly there's a burst of raucous laughter, lots of people guffawing at some joke that I can't quite make out. Am I the joke?

I try to move my arms and legs, but I am imprisoned in some type of device that feels like old-fashioned wooden stocks, facing forward with my wrists held at the level of my locked-in neck. I am sitting on some kind of stool, I think, and my ankles are strapped in cold, steel leg irons, fastened to what must be bolts in the floor about eighteen inches apart. I've no idea what's going to happen to me, and although it's exciting, I think I've had enough sexual adventure for one night. I don't know exactly what my friend raved about, but this is really too much. "I want out," I say, but although I raise my voice and say it again I cannot make myself heard over the din. Of course, since it's my fantasy, I really want no such thing.

Suddenly there's a flurry of activity and a drumroll. I feel heat on my body, like a bright light has been turned on, bathing me in its glare, but I can't see anything through my well-applied blindfold. I would scream but that would be embarrassing, since I did volunteer for whatever this is. As I gather a breath to speak, a loud, announcer-type voice says, "Ladies and gentlemen, may I have your attention?" The room quiets. "For your entertainment tonight, we have another unique show. Max is here, with a living toy to play with. So let's give him a big hand. Let's hear it for Max!"

There is loud applause and more than a few whistles, and I hear movement beside me. "Good evening, everyone." The powerful voice comes from just beside my right ear. "Are you having fun so far?" A cheer rises to almost deafening proportions and a few people stomp their feet. A rowdy group to be sure. "That's good, but

now I have something even better for you. I give you Marnie."
More applause. That's my name all right, and I sense that he truly
means *give you*. I'm afraid, but also very aroused.

"Now, my dear," he says, I assume to me, "let me explain what
you cannot see. You are in Club Ecstasy. Everyone here is free to
do whatever they like, whenever they like, to just about whomever
they like. Some of the men out there are naked; some of the
women are in chains. It's all in fun, of course, fun for everyone.
Are you having fun?" He slaps me on my thigh.

"No," I snap. "I'm not having fun and I want to get out of
here. I've had just about enough." I love protesting in my dream,
knowing there's nothing I can do to change the scenario. That's
one of the best parts.

"You wanted something truly unusual and now you're going to
get it. Frankly I don't care whether you want it or not."

"I want out. Now!" The excitement is almost unbearable, but I
like to fight it.

"I would be very quiet if I were you," Max says, his breath hot
in my ear. "You're in no position to argue, and if you keep yam-
mering I'm going to have to gag you."

"You can't do that. I won't permit it." I know it's a deliberate
dare and I do it on purpose.

Suddenly a penis-shaped piece of plastic is shoved in my mouth
and held in place with a strap around my head. "That's better,"
Max says. "Now, you may nod in answer to my questions. Are you
in any real physical discomfort? Be honest now."

I want to nod yes, but truly I'm not uncomfortable. Just a bit
humiliated. I shake my head.

"That's excellent." A hand slips between my thighs and sweeps
along my crack. I want to pull my knees together to avoid his
questing fingers but the chains hold me in place. "She's very wet,
ladies and gentlemen."

There's a lot of applause and hooting. Why did he have to say that? The fact that I'm aroused is my secret. I slump. I guess it isn't my secret anymore. I decide to go along with it all, not that I have any choice. The total loss of control is what makes this fantasy so hot for me.

As I relax my shoulders Max says, "I see you've finally accepted all this. That's good. Let's give them a good show."

I feel the apparatus holding my head and hands move until I'm pulled upward to a standing position, my feet spread by the manacles on my ankles. A large sheet of some kind of cold plastic is pressed against my chest, forcing my breasts through openings. "Who will suck her?" Max asks, and there's shouting from the audience. "You and you," he says, and quickly two mouths are on my nipples. I can do nothing as small shards of pleasure shoot through me.

"And who wants her pussy?" Again there's noise and soon there are fingers playing between my legs, then a mouth fastens on my clit and begins a rhythmic sucking. It's all incredibly exciting, not knowing who's doing what to my body. "Don't let her come yet," Max says. All the men using me are quite good at it, and soon I can feel the orgasm building. It seems rooted in my legs, trying to flow into my snatch, but the men ministering to me seem able to keep me just on the edge of climax. The mouth on my clit is replaced with fingers manipulating my inner lips and flicking in and out of my channel.

"Now watch this, ladies and gentlemen," Max says. Then the voice is in my ears. "Just so you know, Marnie, I'm focusing a video camera on your cunt, watching the fingers play with you. There are several large TV screens so everyone can share your experience."

His words arouse me even more, but still I can't quite achieve orgasm. "Everyone's watching, my dear," he says loudly. "Everyone will know when you come, with anonymous strangers sucking your tits and playing with your cunt. Everyone will know how hot you are, and later they will all have you, if they want." The fingers play me like some fine instrument, drawing responses from me. My knees want to buckle but the support of the stocks keeps me on my feet. "By morning you'll have come so many times you'll lose count of the climaxes. We will have filled every orifice you have a dozen times over."

Who cares about later? I want it now. I want all the orgasms he's promising me. He pulls the penis/gag from my mouth. "Tell everyone you want to come!" he orders loudly. "Tell them you want everything this evening has in store for you. Tell them!"

He slaps my ass and the fingers finally let me come. I scream in my erotic ecstasy. "Give it all to me!"

I'm in my bed, with my fingers working in my crotch. As I come in this fantasy, I come in reality. It's such a powerful dream that it makes me come every time. I think about Darleen and her suggestion that started this fantasy growing in my brain. Maybe I'll take her up on her offer for real some day. For now, however, the idea makes for the best dreams.

Persimmons

❧

"*H*AVE YOU EVER EATEN A PERSIMMON?" ANNE ASKED HER
friend Janet as she put a plastic grocery bag on the counter. The
two women were going to spend the evening together seeing a
movie, but Anne had needed a few things at the store so she'd
asked her friend to use the key she'd given her, make herself comfortable and wait for her.

"I don't think so."

"I found some ripe ones at the A&P and I bought a few. Try
one." Anne handed Janet a small deep orange fruit, soft to the touch
and smooth skinned. "I've had them before and they're very sensual."

Janet bit through the thick skin and into the flesh. "The skin's
sort of bitter," she said, "but the inside is really sweet. Delicious.
And such an unusual texture."

"It feels like licking a woman's pussy," Anne said, putting a con-
tainer of milk and a six-pack in the refrigerator. "The rest can wait
until tomorrow."

"How the hell would you know about what a woman feels

like?" Janet asked, dropping onto the sofa and putting her feet on the coffee table in the small apartment. The two women were graduate students at a Midwestern university. They had met the first day of the semester when they'd moved into their separate apartments in the same building and had become fast friends. Janet took another bite of the fruit.

"Oh," Anne said with a wink, "I've been around."

Janet sat bolt upright. "Do you mean to tell me that you've been with a woman?" Her jaw almost fell open. "I thought you were a devoted heterosexual."

"Oh damn, now I've shocked you. What the hell. Yes, I've been with a woman from time to time, but I major in men." When Janet didn't immediately respond, Anne grinned and quickly added, "It doubles the chance of a date on Saturday night."

"Don't get flip with me. You're serious."

Anne's face straightened. "Of course I'm serious. I guess I didn't want you to know, but then again, it's who I am."

"You're a lesbian." Janet was surprised at how shocked she was. And titillated. Like many women she'd had her moments of curiosity about what it would be like to be with a woman, but she'd never dared try to find out.

"There aren't just two ways to be, hetero- and homosexual. For me, and for many of the women I've been with, it's a continuum, from only having sex with men to only having sex with women. I'm somewhere in the middle, more toward the hetero end. But I've had some great times with women too." Anne stopped talking abruptly and bit into her persimmon.

"Is this really what a woman feels like?" Janet asked softly, stroking the flesh of the fruit with her tongue. It was soft, juicy and sort of slithery.

Anne closed her eyes and licked the orange fruit. "Yeah, sort of." She licked again. "But a woman feels even nicer. Curious?"

Faced with the sudden question, Janet's mind boggled. She didn't know what to say, or even what to think. Anne was wandering into dangerous territory and Janet didn't know whether she wanted to wander with her. She should just change the topic, and knowing Anne as she did, she knew her friend wouldn't push it. However . . . "Maybe just a little."

"I don't want to push you into anything you're not sure of." There was a sudden sensuous aura around her as she bit into the fruit again. "Our friendship is important to me, and if something goes wrong here we might never be able to look each other in the eye again. That would be a big loss for me."

"Me too," Janet said, realizing that what Anne was saying echoed her feelings. She took a deep breath and let it out slowly. "It scares me, but I have to tell you that I'm also getting very horny."

Grinning, Anne said, "I'd love to give you a lesson in a woman's anatomy, namely mine."

Janet knew she was out on a very slender limb, but now that she was here she had to know. "I don't know whether I want to kiss a woman, though," she said honestly.

"That's okay. I wasn't sure about that at first either. May I touch you?"

After a long pause Janet nodded, rested her head on the back of the sofa and closed her eyes.

Anne laughed. "Don't want to watch? If you have to pretend I'm a guy, let's not do this."

"I guess I want to begin slowly."

"Fair enough."

With her eyes closed Janet felt Anne's hand on her shoulder, stroking and kneading her through her blouse. She didn't pretend the hand belonged to a guy, but neither did she focus on the fact that it was Anne's. She just went with the feelings.

Anne's soft fingertips slid along the side of Janet's neck and then combed through her hair. "Men never think to do this," Anne whispered into her ear as she stroked her friend's scalp. Janet felt Anne shift positions so she was facing her, then straddle her thighs. Now both of Anne's hands were free to caress her neck, face, ears and scalp. *Caress.* Janet thought about that word and realized that few of her previous dates had been so tender.

Then the hands wandered down her breast bone and swirled around the fullness of her breasts. It was almost dizzying, one hand clockwise, one counterclockwise. She felt her nipples harden, and Anne's fingers found them both. "I've always wanted to have big nipples like yours," she said, flicking a fingernail over one bud. "Mine are so small, even erect."

Janet opened her eyes, and her gaze immediately traveled to her friend's breasts. She did have small nipples, but it was obvious from the way they stuck out that she was aroused.

Anne took Janet's hands in hers and raised a questioning eyebrow. Janet nodded and Anne put Janet's hands on her breasts. Her palms filled with the first breasts other than her own she'd ever touched. Janet's focus turned to the feel of her friend's small, hard tips against her skin. She again closed her eyes and slid her hands slowly lower until she could hold those breasts in her hands.

Quickly Anne pulled her shirt over her head and unfastened her bra. "It will feel better without any clothes between us." She pulled Janet's blouse and bra off until the two women were both naked to the waist. They fondled each other, and Janet was surprised at how good it felt. Anne's hands were soft and smooth and seemed to know just how to touch, how hard to scratch.

Janet trembled, her breathing labored, her heart pounding in her chest. She felt her pussy twitch and tiny spasms of pleasure shoot through her body. How they got completely naked she didn't quite know, but then Anne was crouched on the floor between her spread knees, fingers exploring her slit. "Feel good?" Anne asked.

Janet was reluctant to say how much, but this was her best friend after all. "Yes," she whispered. "It really does."

"I can make it feel even better," Anne said, "if it's all right with you. I don't want to take this too far."

"It's not too far," Janet said, barely able to make her lips form the words.

"Mmm," Anne purred, fingers finding Janet's clit. "Right here." Currents of pure erotic pleasure knifed through her as Anne's fingers rubbed the center of her pleasure. Then one finger parted her inner lips and slowly slid inside as Anne's mouth found her mound and her tongue flicked over her clit. Janet tried to hold back but the orgasm was too close, too strong. With a long moan she came, Anne's finger inside her, her mouth sucking at her clit.

The two women rested silently for several minutes. "I'm really close," Anne said, stretching out on the carpet. "I would love it if you'd help me, but I can do it myself if you'd rather not."

Janet had caught her breath, hardly able to fathom what had just happened. "I wouldn't know what to do," Janet said, wanting to give her friend the kind of pleasure she'd just had.

Anne was panting and her hands shook. "Do the things you like to have done to you and I'll tell you if something doesn't work for me. How's that?"

"It's scary."

"Then don't do it," Anne said. "It's not necessary."

"I know." She slipped to the floor and touched Anne's breasts as she had before.

"Too late for teasing. I need you between my legs." She took Janet's hand and put it on her mound. "Just explore. I'll tell you what feels good."

Janet looked at her friend's pussy, framed by her white thighs.

Her pussy hair was as red as the hair on her head and her clit was prominent, poking through her friend's swollen lips. Janet had never touched anything like this before, so wet and slippery, so she did what she liked to have done to her. She explored, finding the crevices and then slowly sliding one finger into the opening. "Oh God," Anne said, her voice hoarse and gravelly. "That's so good. Rub my slit with your other hand." She made small moaning sounds and her hips rocked slightly.

Janet was so curious that, instead of her hand, she touched her friend's clit with the tip of her tongue. The taste was slightly salty, and she recognized the aroma as the way she herself smelled after sex. Anne came then; a long groan punctuated by small screams filled Janet's ears.

A long time later, when the two women could speak again, Anne said, "I hope you won't regret this later."

"I won't. I don't know whether it will ever happen again, but I certainly won't regret it."

Anne smiled. "I'm glad."

Janet started to laugh. "Oh, and you do feel like a persimmon." Anne's laughter joined hers. The two women were still best friends.

Dirty Talking

It STARTED LATE ONE NIGHT IN THE HEAT OF PASSION. Don and Betsy were in bed making love as they had done at least twice a week for the three months they had been living together. Betsy lay beneath him, wet, obviously hot and hungry for his body. As he rose on his elbows, he looked at her, and with the small part of his brain that still worked, he thought that she was the most wonderful woman he'd ever been with. They were interested in the same sports, enjoyed the same movies, loved computer games, basically just had fun together. He loved making love with her, but there was one small difficulty. Betsy was just a little too straight for him. Sure, she performed oral sex on him and seemed to enjoy it when he did the same to her, but there was something missing. There was no real spark, no heat, no real passion. He wanted her to be as heated as he was. Sinking back into his erotic haze, without thinking he whispered, "God, how I love fucking you."

Before he could thrust into her, he felt Betsy tense, and coming to his senses, he realized what he'd done. Betsy never cursed, never used the kind of Anglo-Saxon four-letter words that Don used with his male friends, and he'd refrained from using such language with her. Now he'd gone and done it; he'd said *fuck*.

He drew back, ready to apologize, sure their evening of sex, and maybe their relationship, was over. But hell, this was who he was, a little rough around the edges but a pretty good guy. He was totally surprised, however, when conventional Betsy pulled him close, wrapped her legs around his buttocks and almost pulled him inside of her. After only a few thrusts, she screamed and came with more enthusiasm than he ever remembered her doing. It took only a few more thrusts for him to climax as well, pounding into Betsy harder than he'd ever done before.

He was amazed. It was as though someone had lit a fire under his usually restrained girlfriend, and that, in turn, had lit a bone-shattering fire beneath him. He loved it when she was an active participant in their passion. *Fuck?* Was it that word that made her so crazy? He rolled off of her, removed his condom and lay on his back, arm bent beneath his head. He wanted to ask her about what had happened but was reluctant to bring it up. He'd wait until the next time they were in bed together and then try to find out whether words aroused her. That is, if he was brave enough.

As if sensing his question, Betsy put her hand on his belly as she lay beside him and said, "That word you used did something to me."

He held his breath, anticipating more, but when she said nothing else, he did what he thought she'd want. "I'm sorry if it offended you," he said, hoping that would provide the opening he'd been waiting for.

"It did, but it didn't." She idly stroked his skin. "This is very difficult to talk about. Words like that . . . I don't know. I've never used them. My family was awfully conservative; my folks never cursed, even at the worst times."

"I know that and I've never used dirty words in front of you. I would never offend or upset you. You know that."

"Of course I do. You never talk during sex."

Before Betsy, Don had often been quite unrestrained with his vocabulary, but with her, he'd been quiet. Now he realized that he missed the heat that dirty talking in bed brought him. He rolled over and propped himself on his elbow. "I've always been afraid to embarrass or upset you. Do you want me to talk when we make love?"

"I don't know." Betsy rolled over, pulled the covers up over both of them and snuggled against him. "I don't know, but what we had this evening was really great."

For the next several days, Don thought about that evening. He was pretty sure that he and Betsy had a long future together. He knew that he loved her and had been considering asking her to marry him. The one thing that had always held him back was their sex life. It was satisfying, but that evening she'd been more aggressive than he'd ever seen her. And he liked it. Maybe there was more to Betsy's appetite than he'd thought.

About a week after that mind-bending, orgasmic evening they'd shared, they returned to their apartment after seeing a movie and settled on the sofa with a bottle of wine to watch the eleven o'clock news. As they watched, they kissed, the kisses growing increasingly hungry. When his hand wandered to Betsy's breast, she moved to provide him better access. Predictably, by the time the news was over they were both breathless and needy. Because of their opposite work schedules, they hadn't had an opportunity to make love since that eye-opening evening, so Don was anticipating good things. He'd even practiced a few choice phrases to whisper in the heat of passion.

In the back of his mind, Don kept reliving Betsy's reaction to his use of the word *fucking*, so as he unhooked her bra, he said,

"You've got great tits." Again she tensed, but she moved closer, took his hand and put it on her breast. She had never been the initiator before. *Interesting. Maybe talking dirty gets to her,* he thought, *or maybe it's just talking during sex. Either way* . . . "Great tits," he purred as his mouth found her nipple.

Later, in the bedroom, as he stroked her wet folds, he whispered, "Your body is so beautiful and you're so wet and hot." The sex that followed was better than ever before.

Over the next few weeks, he struggled to find the right things to say during lovemaking. He had often talked during sex with his previous girlfriends, and now he suspected that hot words might be the key to unlocking the much more passionate woman inside Betsy. He said a sentence or two each time, one he'd thought about beforehand and had, in a few cases, even rehearsed on his way home from work.

It worked every time. "I want to fuck you so hard." "I love being inside you."

"Don," Betsy said as they lay side by side in the dark one night, "I wanted to talk to you. About talking." She reached over and tentatively took his hand. He knew her well and knew that talking about sex was just as difficult for her as talking during sex.

He had to help. "I know that my talking during sex excites you, and I love it that you want me like that."

"You really do?"

"Of course I do." He rolled over and kissed her ear. "I love talking dirty to you, and I love what it does for you."

"It's difficult for me to admit that it gets to me."

"I know, baby. I also know that when I say *fuck*, or *tits*, or *pussy*, it makes you crazy." He hastened to add, "In a great way, I mean."

"Thanks for understanding how hard this is."

He put her hand on his erection. "How about how hard this is?"

She giggled. "I like touching you."

Don suddenly suspected that there was something hanging in the air, but he wasn't sure what it was. Then he had an idea. "That's my cock."

"Mmm," Betsy moaned.

Don kissed her deeply, his hand stroking her soft skin. He swirled his fingers around the skin of her breast, careful not to touch her extremely sensitive nipples. When she began to squirm, he whispered, "Do you want me to touch your nipples?"

"Mmm."

"Say it."

"Say what?"

"Say, 'Please touch my nipples.'"

She shuddered and her hands froze on his back. "Touch me," she said after a long pause.

"'Please touch my nipples,'" he repeated. "Say it."

"Please touch me."

A light went on. He remembered a phrase from when he was a kid. She was experiencing delicious fear. Like a kid peeking at a scary movie through his fingers. She wanted to be coaxed to talk dirty to him. If he was right they could spice up their sex life still more, and have fun doing it. He pursued it. "Not good enough," he said, still stroking her breasts. "Say 'Touch my nipples.'"

"Touch my nipples," she said, her voice small and tentative.

He gave her her wish. He slid his palm over the engorged tips of her breasts, then suckled the way he knew she liked it. For long, silent minutes he made love to her body, touching, lightly scratching, softly pinching until he felt fluid flow onto the inside of her thighs. Next step. "Want me to touch your pussy?"

"Yes," she moaned.

"Then ask me." Again he teased, gliding his fingers close to her swollen flesh, grazing her pubic hair, but not touching her where she needed to be touched.

He felt her great sigh. "Touch my"—she hesitated—"pussy."

He found her clit, and it took only a moment's rubbing for her to scream her climax. While she was still pulsing, he drove into her; his orgasm was just as strong as hers.

Later he said, "I guess you didn't mind me forcing you to say those words."

She giggled and held him tightly. "Don't tell anyone, but it was really hot."

He encircled her in his arms. The fun was just beginning.

A Rape Fantasy

✦

$\mathcal{I}$ AWOKE IN THE MIDDLE OF THE NIGHT AS I SOMETIMES DO, hot and hungry. I grabbed the shreds of the erotic dream I'd been having and, in the dark, built a delicious fantasy. It's a violent one, and I would never think of enjoying anything like this in real life, but I love the helpless feeling I have in my dream. I don't have to worry about what to do; it's all being done to me.

In my fantasy I am walking along down a long, deserted country road. It's midsummer and the earth retains the heat of the day. The moon is bright and lights the flat land around me almost as brightly as the sun had earlier. I'm unaware of the three men standing in the shadows, but when they suddenly appear I know what's going to happen and I accept it. The three appear to be in their twenties, good-looking and muscular, their well-developed bodies clearly visible through low-slung, body-hugging jeans and tight, sleeveless muscle shirts.

I'm dressed in a tiny pair of shorts and a cut-off polo shirt that barely covers my large chest. In my fantasy I'm slender, but very well-endowed, ten years younger than my real age, with long, wavy blond hair and deep blue eyes.

When I see the guys heading toward me, my pulse quickens and my breathing speeds up. I'm both afraid and aroused. "Hey, Johnny, this is one prime piece of real estate," one says, staring at my chest. "Great knockers too."

"She sure is built, Mack," the one called Johnny says. "Let's stake a claim." He's blond and shorter than the other two.

"How about it, sweetie?" Mack says through heavy, sensuous lips, his black mustache standing out against his white skin. Diamond studs wink in his ears. "Wanna play?"

"Of course not," I snap back, knowing that nothing I say will change anything. "I'm on my way home and I'm in a hurry. My husband will be waiting for me, and if I'm late, he'll come looking for me."

"Your husband's one lucky guy," Johnny says. "We promise that we won't keep you too long, will we, KJ?"

"Not too long at all." KJ's laugh is deep and has an evil undertone. His eyes are small and placed close together, a look that makes his laugh seem even more sinister. His arms and as much of his upper body as I can see are covered with multicolored tattoos.

Suddenly Johnny grabs one of my wrists and KJ the other, and I'm forced over to the grassy verge and onto my back. "Hold her down," Mack says as he unzips his jeans. "It's my turn to go first."

I struggle and kick, but the men are too much for me. The more I squirm, the tighter they hold my arms and legs until I'm powerless to resist whatever they want to do. I'm incredibly excited by my inability to oppose them. Now Mack has a pair of scissors. I've no idea where they came from, but it's my fantasy so I can create whatever I want. "Don't move or I'm might cut you," he says, the snicking of the blades accenting his words. "Do you hear me?"

Now he's forcing me not only to remain still but also, by

inaction, to be part of what's happening. "Do you hear me?" he says again.

Reluctantly I say, "I hear you."

"Hurry it up, Mack," Johnny says. "I want mine before I'm too old to enjoy it."

"You'll get your turn," Mack says, sliding the cold blade of the scissors beneath my shorts and cutting across the crotch until the fabric parts. I'm wearing no panties, so he's got clear access to my pussy. He rubs me with his fingers. "You're really wet. This all excites you, doesn't it." It's not a question. "Tell me how hot you are."

Again I have to talk. "I don't want this."

"Of course you do, slut. Your pussy is swollen and hot and your juices are running down your snatch. You can't deny it, so stop pretending." He laughs. "Say it," he taunts. "Tell me how hot this all makes you." When I remain silent, he jams his fingers into me and finger fucks my pussy. "Tell me!"

I'm trying to keep my hips from bucking against his hand. I can't tell him how hungry he's making me. He stops fucking me and leans over and flicks his tongue over my clit. "Tell me," he says, "or I'll just let you stay hot and hungry while I jerk off." He unzips, drops his jeans and fondles his large cock. Leering at me, he strokes it from base to head. I want his cock and he knows it. Despite being held down tightly, despite the fact that I'm being raped, I want his cock. "Tell me," he says yet again, "or I'll keep jerking off."

My eyes can't leave his hand, slowly massaging his cock. He leans over and blows on my heated flesh, then lightly rubs the head of his cock through my wetness. In my fantasy diseases and pregnancies don't exist, of course, so there's no need for condoms. I want him to ram it into me. "Yes," I finally say. "Oh, yes."

"Yes, please?"

"Yes, please." I'm almost jibbering with lust. "Do me."

He rams his cock home, filling me until I want to scream from the pleasure of it. He pulls out and thrusts the full length hard into me again. Over and over he fucks me until I'm ready to come. He fills me with his semen first, then pulls out. "Almost came, didn't you?" he teases. "Not yet, baby. There's so much more to come."

He adjusts his position to take over from KJ. "I want your cunt wide-open," he growls, spreading my legs farther and holding my ankles while KJ pulls his jeans down. Knowing I'm too weak to struggle anymore, Johnny lets go. The only hands on my body now are Mack's. "Open your mouth, bitch," Johnny says. "I'm not much of a pussy guy so KJ can have your cunt. You can suck me off."

He holds my nose until I open my mouth. It's funny that he feels he has to do that since I would have sucked his cock just because I love to do it. I guess it makes him feel like he's doing something against my will. I open my mouth and feel his hard, smooth cock invade. I lick and suck while he slides in and out. "Oh, she's a good little cocksucker," he says, his breathing loud and raspy.

KJ is playing with my pussy while Mack squeezes my tits until they hurt. It's difficult to concentrate on Johnny's cock in my mouth with so much pleasure filling my groin. Then I feel a cock fill me again, while fingers play with my nipples. I'm not really sure who's doing what to me anymore, but I don't care. It's all too good and I know I'm going to come. It's almost simultaneous. KJ fills my pussy with his semen while Johnny fills my mouth. One more squeeze of my tit and I explode, colors swirling through my brain.

As I climax in my fantasy, my body reaches its peak and I can feel the spasms on my fingers. Slowly I relax and slip back into sleep.

Petra's New Car

⁂

$\mathcal{U}$NTIL THAT NIGHT, PETRA HAD NEVER REALIZED THAT HER new car would come with such delicious fringe benefits.

She'd only had the car a month and already Petra loved her Honda, with its GPS system, remote starter, leather seats and electric everything. Having never been a "thing" person, she hated to admit that she loved the luxury of it all.

After the first week she'd let her husband drive it and he'd become as enthusiastic about it as she was. Even though Ben drove a top-of-the-line two-year-old Lexus, he and Petra argued from time to time about who got to drive which car.

Late one summer evening they were leaving a party with friends and Petra asked Ben to drive. "I'm a bit buzzed, and since you haven't been drinking, it would be better if you drove."

"Thanks for surrendering your baby," Ben said as he slid onto the slick leather seat and inserted the key in the ignition. "Actually it will be better in a few different ways," Ben said. "I've got a fiendish idea about your car."

Petra's eyebrows climbed as she got into the passenger seat. "What kind of idea?" From the gleam in his eye, she knew his idea was sexual. Her husband had a devious mind, and often his *ideas* had led to wonderful evenings of lovemaking. Sometimes, however, he did tend to go a little further than Petra was totally comfortable with. She wondered what he had in mind tonight—and with her car? What could a car have to do with sex?

"Wait and see, love," he said pulling out of their friends' driveway.

Since the Bannisters, the couple they'd been visiting, lived on the other side of town, the drive home would take almost a half hour, even taking sneaky back roads to avoid traffic. About halfway home, Petra's curiosity finally got the better of her. "Okay, what's your fiendish idea?" He'd piqued her curiosity, and she was both intrigued and a little worried.

"I think you should take your panties off."

"What?" With all the windows and the sunroof open there was a warm breeze through the car and it was almost like being outdoors. There was only a quarter moon so it was dim but not totally dark inside.

Ben turned onto a back street and slowed to about thirty miles an hour. "You heard me. Take your panties off and put them on the backseat."

Not totally sure how she felt about being so open about sex, she stalled for time. "Why?"

"Why not?" Ben's teeth gleamed in the dim light as he grinned at her. When she hesitated, he continued. "No one can see anything, darling, and it sounds like a kick to me."

"Sure." She giggled in spite of herself. "You're not the one who'd have her ass hanging out."

"Come on. Be a sport. I think you'll be in for a thrill."

Petra thought about it and decided that Ben was probably

192 BAWDY BEDTIME STORIES

right. It was totally private in the car. And anyway, maybe she was
a bit of a prude when it came to sex. What the hell. She was slightly
tipsy and, if she was honest with herself, willing to try something
new and erotic. She unfastened her seat belt and began wriggling
out of her undies. Luckily she'd worn a full skirt so she easily
pulled her panties down. "Okay," she said, flipping the bit of nylon
into the back and refastening her seat belt. "Does the idea of my
being naked beneath my skirt excite you?"

"It does," Ben said, slowing further, now doing only twenty-
five. "Now pull up the back of your skirt until your bare bottom is
on the leather."

"I don't want to mess up the new upholstery," Petra protested.
What the heck did he have in mind?

"The leather can stand it," Ben said. "Be a good girl and do it
because I asked you to."

Tired of being so uptight, and excited by Ben's authoritative
tone, Petra threw caution to the wind, lifted her hips within the
confines of the seat belt and slid the fabric of her skirt up behind
her. As her hot skin touched the cool leather, she jumped. "Yikes,
that's cold," she said.

"Not for long," Ben said, reaching over and flipping the switch
to turn on the seat heater. After a few moments, Petra felt warmth
on her flesh. Her nether lips had never been exposed to anything
like that heat before.

"How does it feel?" Ben asked.

Reluctant to let Ben know how much the heat on her parts
excited her, she kept her voice bland and merely said, "It feels
warm."

Ben glanced over. "Your nipples say different. Your nipples say
your bottom likes the heat and it is making you hot all over."

It did make her hot; she could feel her flesh swelling and moistening. Why not tell Ben? It wasn't dirty, was it?

"How about pulling your top up so those tight little nips of yours can feel the air?"

This was going too far. Wasn't it? Someone might be out walking a dog or coming home late from a party. They'd see her bare breasted.

As if reading her mind, Ben said, "No one can see into the car. Since there's only a sliver of a moon it's almost pitch-black in here, and there are no streetlights in this part of town."

"I don't know. It feels naughty."

"In this case *naughty* isn't that far from delightful. Get a little crazy. Feel the heat on your pretty little pussy and the cool on your tits."

Recently Ben had begun using dirty language and Petra was reluctant to admit, even to herself, how much it excited her. Now she felt her parts twitch. She rested her head against the headrest, closed her eyes and sighed.

"Nipples don't lie," Ben said, "and yours are so tight I bet they hurt a little."

They did. Resigned, she pulled up the knit fabric of her top and felt the summer breeze on her flesh. "Oh my God," she said. She felt shards of excitement rocket through her.

"Such beautiful breasts," Ben purred. "I can see them even in the dark."

If he could see them, then anyone walking by could too. She ought to be scandalized, but she realized that she was too hungry to worry about it.

"Touch them. Play with your nipples while I watch."

"I couldn't," she choked out.

"They want you to, and your fingers are itching for it too. I know it and so do you. Do it so I can watch."

She swallowed hard. Her fingers did want it, and her nipples were so tight they hurt. "You should keep your eyes on your driving."

"Don't worry about my driving," Ben said, softly. "Touch. Rub your palms over the tips. Just that."

Slowly she raised her hands and stroked her palms across her engorged nipples. It felt incredibly erotic. She was touching her breasts in the open air. She could feel the breeze, although it had lessened to just a whisper. She opened her eyes. Ben had pulled the car over so it sat at the curb, idling. He was staring at her, smiling. "Like that," he whispered, unfastening her seat belt. "Touch them just like that."

For long moments she rubbed herself, then she felt Ben's hand over hers, cupping her fingers and pressing against her breast flesh. "Yes," he breathed. "You look so beautiful stroking your skin in the moonlight." He flipped the visor on her side down and exposed the lighted mirror. "Look at how beautiful."

There was just enough light to illuminate her hands, tanned against her white skin. She closed her eyes but still she could see the sensual image of her fingers spread on her breasts.

Silence stretched in the car with Ben's hand now resting on her shoulder. Then he reached across the gearshift lever and pulled up her skirt until it was bunched against her belly, exposing her thighs. "Right here," he said, insinuating his finger through her pubic hair to find her swollen clit. "This is where you want to be touched. Right here."

She did want it, very much. She parted her thighs, hands still on her breasts. "Yes." She sighed.

"Not me, you. Touch yourself so I can watch."

She masturbated many times while Ben was away on business trips, but she'd never done it when Ben might be aware. She felt her body stiffen and her fingers tighten as if to keep themselves from doing something so naughty. "I can't."

"Of course you can. I'm sure you do it when I'm not around, and I don't mind a bit. So why not do it now?"

She shook her head slightly.

"Please, show me. I want to watch. With the heat on your pussy and the cool on your tits you must be getting ready to come. Touch yourself and let yourself climax. Show me everything."

She couldn't. Ben took one hand gently and placed it low on her belly. "Slide it down just a little bit. You know you want to. Do it for me."

She allowed her fingers to slip lower. She wanted it so much. Ben's fingers stroked the inside of her thighs above the tops of her stockings, making her want to squirm closer. "You do it," she moaned.

"Not me. If you want that gigantic itch scratched, you'll have to do it yourself. Please."

She slid her fingers through her hair until she found her clit. Almost as if they had a mind of their own they fondled, teased, rubbed her flesh until she was so high she didn't care who was watching. Then, as she rubbed, Ben's fingers glided through the wetness and into her. She couldn't resist the building climax, nor did she want to. She let it break over her like a tidal wave, crashing onto her, flooding her with the most unbelievable pleasure. On and on the waves came until she was drained.

Heart pounding, barely able to breathe, she felt Ben's fingers slip from her. When she could function again, she pulled her shirt down and covered her lap with her skirt.

"That was amazing," Ben said.

"It was, and then some," she admitted.

"I've never been able to watch your face as you come. There's such joy there. Why do you ever deny yourself all that pleasure?"

Petra thought about it. Was being more reserved about sex denying herself? Maybe it was. "How about you?" she said, realizing that Ben hadn't gotten his pleasure. "You didn't . . ."

"I got so much joy from just watching you that it's okay. Maybe when we get home."

Maybe right now, she thought. *Right here, right now.* She reached over and unzipped his trousers and opened the fly of his shorts, drawing his rigid member into the open air. She'd performed oral sex on him many times, but never in public like this. "How does the air feel on you?"

"It's erotic," he groaned, letting his head fall back onto the headrest. "You don't have to do this, you know."

"I know," she said, leaning over the gearshift lever and taking him in her hand. He was so hard she could feel the pulse of his need. She could do this, right here. She bent lower and licked the end of his cock, tasting the precome that oozed from the tip. She lapped, allowing her tongue to dip lower down his shaft with each stroke. Soon she was licking the length of him and knowing he was having a difficult time keeping still.

Then she opened her mouth and took the head of his erection in her mouth as she wrapped her fingers around the shaft. Squeezing and sucking, she felt spasms shake him. "Don't," he said. "I won't be able to hold back."

"So let go." She didn't want him to come in her mouth, so when she felt his climax approach she kept running one hand up and down his penis while she grabbed a handful of tissues from the console with the other. His head pressed back and his body went rigid, then he spurted, moaning long and low. She caught all of his semen in the tissues.

Later, as they both rearranged their clothing, she said, "I'm sorry but I didn't want you to come in my mouth."

"I can't imagine anything you would need to apologize for. It was absolutely wonderful. If at some point you want me to ejaculate in your mouth, that would be fabulous. If not, that's all right too."

It slowly dawned on Petra what they'd just done and she was shocked at herself. "I can't believe what we just did."

"I can't either, but let's think about doing it again."

Petra looked around at the split-level houses, most darkened. "Maybe not in such a public place."

"Maybe, maybe not. Let's hear it for heated seats," Ben said, turning the switch off. "I do love your new car."

All Petra could do was let out a long "Yeah."

The Prince's Sorcerer

𝓛ORBAN WAS CROWN PRINCE JUSTIN'S SORCERER AND served him well, as he did the prince's father, King Marcus. He cast spells to bring rain to the kingdom, improve the crops and fill the forests with game. He guaranteed fertility to the royal family: King Marcus and his queen had been blessed with seven sons and three daughters. Several of Prince Justin's brothers and sisters already had happy marriages and very large families.

Prince Justin had been very selective, however, and had waited until he was well past thirty to choose a bride. Finally, four years before, the prince had returned from a trip to a neighboring kingdom and had brought back a lovely, quiet lady to be the future queen. The marriage had been the event to end all events; the celebratory parties had lasted for several weeks.

Princess Elaine had quickly blessed the kingdom with twins, Princes Frederick and Ewan, and then Princess Marian. With succession secure, life in the kingdom settled down to routine.

One afternoon the prince visited Lorban's workroom in the

castle basement. After a bit of small talk, the prince seemed to hesi-
tate. "Sire?" the sorcerer said. "Is there something you want from
me?"

"Well," the prince said, his face reddening, "it's about the
princess."

"Is Princess Elaine unwell?" Lorban asked, suddenly worried.
If the princess was ill he should have already known it. "Is there
something I can do to help?"

The prince immediately reassured his sorcerer. "No, no. She's
quite well." He smiled hesitantly. "And the children as well. Everyone's fine. We're all just fine." He patted the older man on the hand
and stood, his face slightly flushed.

Lorban knew Prince Justin well enough to know that something was definitely bothering him, so when the prince turned to
leave without discussing what he'd come to talk about, Lorban
stopped him. "Sire, something is obviously bothering you. Why
don't we have a cup of tea and we can talk about other things until
you're ready to tell me about it?"

Quickly Lorban brewed a cup of a special blend of tea, filled
with herbs to help the prince relax and loosen his tongue. Of
course, the prince knew nothing about the power of the herbs. After a few sips, Lorban watched the prince's shoulders relax and his
back rest against the chair's cushions. With a deep breath, the
prince said, "It's about, well, well, the bedroom. I'm afraid I'm not
satisfying the princess with regard to, well, marital relations."

"I'm so sorry to hear that, sire."

"Yes, yes," the prince said, dropping his chin and fanning his face.
A side effect of the herbs was the heating of the blood. "Well, I'm
afraid I just don't know how to please her. Now that succession is
out of the way, I'd like to enjoy time with the princess, but it has become quite frustrating. I spend a great deal of time worrying about
what I should do for her, and I don't, well, get too much pleasure."

"You don't think you're making her happy. Is that it?"

"That's exactly it. Things are comfortable and friendly, but the spark that we once had is gone, and I don't think she, well, reaches her peak anymore."

"Have you talked to her, sire? Has she told you anything?"

"Of course not. You know the princess. She's so quiet and loving. I just wish I knew what she was thinking, what she wants."

"Let me consider this problem, your majesty, and I'll see what I can come up with."

Later that day, Lorban found the princess in her chambers and hoped he could get her to confide in him. "My lady," he said, "it's nice to have a chance to talk with you. We don't see each other often enough anymore."

"It's lovely to see you, Lorban." She motioned him to a chair.

"Thank you, my lady. I've taken the liberty of bringing a pot of my specially blended tea. May I pour you a cup?"

After several sips of the special herbs, the princess's hands relaxed and a fine sheen of perspiration covered her brow. Lorban had thought for quite a while of the right words. "Your highness," he said, "I know how much you love your husband."

"Oh, yes," she said softly, smiling a small contented smile. "He's such a wonderful man, and a great prince as well."

"And the children are such a delight for you both. It must be a pleasure not to be 'with child' anymore."

She grinned and patted her tiny waist. "Oh, most certainly."

"Are you and the prince happy with your nighttime activities in general?" Lorban would not normally have dared to the princess such a direct question, but with his special tea he was sure that she wouldn't be offended.

"He doesn't seem to be getting as much pleasure as he used to, and I'm afraid I'm to blame. Our lovemaking has become quite ordinary. I'd like us to try something new."

"Do you have something special in mind, your highness?"

She smiled. "I'd like to try a few new things, but it simply doesn't happen."

"Have you talked to the prince about it?"

"Of course not. He's a wonderful man and I would never suggest anything that might distress him. He thinks things are just fine as they are, and I would never hint that that they were otherwise."

Later in his chambers, Lorban thought about the problem. Each of the royals was dissatisfied and for the same reason. They just couldn't communicate. He could try to discuss it with them either together or separately, but he'd rather not openly butt in. As he dwelled on the problem, he had an idea. He wondered whether his special herbs might do the trick. He could put some in a carafe of wine in an effort to help two people he cared so deeply about improve their love life. Yes, he reasoned, it might just work.

Later that week, Lorban ground several small scoops of the herbs into a very fine powder and let them steep in a decanter of the prince and princess's favorite Cabernet. That evening he substituted the contents of his bottle for the wine in the royal decanter in the couple's bedroom, then settled himself in an antechamber and peered through a peephole he'd discovered many years before.

The royal couple had dismissed their entire retinue, and the prince poured a glass of ruby wine for his wife, then one for himself. They sipped as they sat in soft chairs and read. "It's such a lovely night," the prince said, looking up from his book. He'd just finished his first glass of wine. "Why don't we open the windows and enjoy the spring air?"

The princess swallowed the last few drops in her glass. "That sounds like a wonderful idea. It's getting a bit warm in here and the fresh breeze should be quite cooling."

Lorban smiled. Things were progressing smoothly.

"I'm finding it a bit warm as well. I think I'll take off these heavy outer clothes." The prince removed his jacket and doublet, then refilled their glasses. "That's much better. Dear, why don't you take off some of those heavy layers too?"

"Yes, I think I shall." As Lorban peered through the opening, the princess removed her outer clothing until she was dressed only in her camisole and pantaloons. "Ah, yes, this is indeed better."

"Come over to the window," the prince said. "There's a festival with music and dancing going on in the square."

Looking down at the happy crowd, the princess said, "Remember when we used to dance?" She held her arms out to her husband. "Let's do it now."

The prince cleared his throat. Usually, Lorban knew, he was a bit too stuffy for such activities, but with the herbs . . .

"I think that's a wonderful idea." He took the princess in his arms and began to waltz her around the chamber. Finally, after several dances, the couple collapsed onto the bed, breathless. "That was so much fun, my dear," he said. He retrieved their wine and each took a sizable drink.

"There are lots more fun things we can do," the princess said.

"Like what?"

"Like kissing. We don't kiss the way we used to."

"We can certainly change that." The prince gazed down at his wife, his fingers stroking her cheek. "Let's change a lot of things." Then he touched his lips to hers and smoothed her hair from her temples. They kissed until they were both breathing heavily, the princess's arms wrapped around the prince's shoulders, kneading his back.

As Lorban watched, the prince kissed his way down the side of his wife's neck, then down her breastbone. The princess's fingers tangled in her husband's hair and a delighted smile lit her face.

Then the prince pulled down his wife's camisole and took one fully erect nipple in his mouth. He drew it in, then echoed his mouth's caresses on her other breast.

Lorban could see the gleam of moisture on the princess's skin, and his own growing heat caused him to slip his robe from his shoulders. He thought about how wrong it was to be such a voyeur, but he had ceased caring. Originally he had merely wanted to know whether his plan had worked, but now it had become too erotic a scene for him to look away.

"Oh, your highness," the princess said with a grin, "you haven't lost your touch." As the prince crouched over her, the princess reached between his legs and cupped his testicles. She lightly kneaded his sac, then tenderly caressed the area between his sac and his anus.

"Neither have you, my dear," the prince groaned.

They played, fondling each other as they hadn't in many years. Finally they were naked. "Do you remember the way we did it once or twice long ago?" the princess asked, lifting herself onto all fours.

"I do indeed," the prince said.

Watching the prince's royal staff play with the princess's beautiful cleft, Lorban pulled out his erect cock and began to stroke it.

The prince held his erection and used the tip to rub the princess's clit as she cried out in ecstasy. "Do it!" she yelled.

"You mean like this?" he said, ramming his phallus into her from behind.

"Yes," she shrieked. "Like that."

While the prince reached around to stroke his wife's clit, she extended her arm between her legs and compressed his sac. Lorban couldn't take his eyes away from the scene in the bedchamber as the rhythm of his own hand increased.

"Like that!" she cried, then screamed her pleasure.

Lorban came in his hand as the prince climaxed in his wife's passage. It was all the sorcerer could do to stifle the noises he himself made. Fortunately there was too much noise from the bedchamber for anyone to notice.

Later he slipped from the antechamber and walked swiftly back to his own rooms. Three members of the royal household were satisfied that night, and like his friends the prince and princess, Lorban quickly fell asleep with a satisfied smile on his face.

A Pool Party

⚜

THE PARTY WAS IN FULL SWING, AND I DO MEAN SWING, when Bret and I arrived in the lush backyard of our friends Connie and Mike. Several couples lay in lounge chairs around the Swansons' big inground pool, talking, while others paddled around in the water or relaxed in the hot tub. Several couples were slow dancing on the deck. While no one was messy drunk, everyone seemed delightfully mellow. Someone handed me a margarita and I downed it in only a few swallows. The Swansons really did know how to throw a party.

I knew from previous occasions that the guests would be a mix of straights and gays, swingers and those, like Bret and me, who weren't really interested in swapping. The more adventurous guests kept their activities private from those of us who weren't into it, but we always knew what was going on. Maybe, eventually, I might be interested, and I knew Bret was. However, he wouldn't do anything unless I was going to indulge also, and he knew that time hadn't come yet.

I quickly removed my polo shirt and shorts, revealing my new bathing suit beneath. I'm not gorgeous by any means, and I've got about fifteen pounds I've been trying unsuccessfully to lose for at least a year. With stretch marks from my two pregnancies, I wasn't too keen on revealing too much, so I'd bought something the website called a tankini. It was a black and yellow floral-print two-piece; the top resembled the top of a tank suit, with a full bra beneath, and the bikini-style bottoms had strings that tied on the side, making bows on each hip. Sexy but not revealing—and it covered my thick waist.

Frankly I thought I didn't look half bad since the long top held in my extra pounds. "Hey, Wendy," called a guy I knew from previous Swanson parties, "you look great." He patted the lounge chair beside him. "Come sit with me. Maybe we could fool around. Bret could either watch or find his own lady." It was said in a light, joking tone, but I knew that the guy would jump at the chance if I agreed. It was flattering, but I didn't quite know how to react to such a direct invitation. Usually the swingers at the Swansons' parties were a bit more subtle and considerate. He'd probably had a bit too much to drink, and I was pretty sure that Mike or Connie would talk with him about it.

"Maybe later," Bret said, waving the guy off and squeezing my hand. "Wanna go in the hot tub, babe?"

I sighed with relief. "Sure." Bret got me another drink and together we climbed into the warm, swirling water. The bubbles kept me from seeing below the water's surface, so I stepped in carefully, then lowered myself into the sensuously heated froth. Bret settled beside me and we held hands.

We introduced ourselves to another couple already in the spa. It turned out that we had mutual friends with Angie and Frank, and we easily got to talking. A short while later someone handed me yet a third drink, and as I sipped I realized that I was nicely buzzed.

Bret reached for another drink for himself, and as he did so, his arm brushed across my breasts. It felt really sexy and I found I wanted more. I slid closer, and as we talked, I draped my arm over the rim of the tub and idly stroked his shoulder. He wiggled toward me, and as I slid over to allow him room, I realized that he'd maneuvered me so that one of the spa's jets pounded my back, and bubbles tickled the insides of my thighs. It all felt wonderful and sort of sensual.

"You guys watch TV," Frank said. "Angie and I missed last week's episode of *Lost*. Did you happen to see it?"

"Sure," I said and began to go through the machinations of the castaways on the island. As I rambled, I felt Bret's hand on my thigh. Sotto voce, he said, "Just keep talking."

Not sure what he meant, I finished the story.

"I just love that show," Angie said. "Do you watch *House*?"

"I think he's a thoroughly rotten person," I said, feeling Bret's hand sliding up the inside of my thigh, "and I feel really sorry for those doctors who work with him, but I can't help watching."

"Me neither," Angie said, "but Frank could care less."

"Bret too," I said. Beneath the water Bret's other hand found my nipple and tweaked it. It was all I could do not to react, but I kept my cool. I didn't want Frank or Angie to know what was going on. I tried to push Bret's hand away, but each time I succeeded he just found a new spot to rub. I found I couldn't deal with both his hands, so I began to try to ignore his caresses. Fat chance.

"What about *CSI*?" Angie asked. "Did you see the one . . . ?"

Angie's voice faded as Bret's fingers found my pussy through the crotch of my suit. I could barely follow what Angie was saying, but I tried to look interested while Bret caressed me. He knew my rhythm and fondled my clit through my bikini bottom until I was being driven crazy.

Angie turned to her husband. "I just loved the last *CSI: New York*. That was the one . . ."

Fortunately the couple seemed to be talking more to each other than to us so I could stop trying to concentrate on their conversation and deal with Bret. As I turned toward him, I felt his fingers untie the sides of my tankini bottom and pull it aside. He quickly found my slippery channel and filled me with three fingers.

"Bret," I hissed, "stop it."

"Not a chance," he said, his fingers sawing in and out. "But you can't come. You know how you scream, and if you do, everyone will know what's going on here."

Knowing he was right, I bit the inside of my lip to tamp down my excitement. "So cut it out," I whispered.

"Nope. I want to see how high I can get you when you can't come." He pulled his fingers out and began to stroke my clit. It's a maneuver guaranteed to push me over the edge. But I couldn't. I just couldn't climax right here, sitting in a hot tub with another couple watching.

"Do you watch that one?" Angie asked lightly, obviously oblivious to what was going on.

"I'm sorry," I said, "I guess I must have drifted away." I swallowed hard, trying not to scream. "Which show?"

"*Cold Case*. It's on Sunday. I really prefer the shows like that, ones that solve a case in each episode."

"Me too," I said, pushing Bret's hand away, to no avail. "The continued ones . . ."

"I know exactly what you mean," Angie said.

"What about *Lost*?" Frank said. "That's continued."

Again they were talking to each other and I tried to scooch a little ways away from Bret, but he was having none of it. "Don't try to get up," he whispered, his Cheshire cat grin lighting his tanned face. "The bottom of your suit is totally untied. If you move you'll lose it completely."

I reached down and grabbed the strings of my bikini while Bret's fingers kept up their play. I could feel my erect nipple rub against the inside of my top as Bret's palm rubbed one beneath the bubbling water. I couldn't deal with his ministrations much longer and we both knew it.

"I'm going to get out soon," Bret said. He pulled one hand from the bubbles and stared at it, the other still playing with my clit. How could he seem so calm? "I'm starting to get wrinkly. You guys have been in here longer than we have. Aren't you getting pruney?"

"Yeah," Frank said, "and I need another drink."

"Me too," I croaked, nearly crazed with lust and the need to climax.

Bret chimed in, "Why don't you two find us a place to sit and we'll be along in a moment? Know where the towels are?" He sounded so normal. I gritted my teeth.

"I saw a stack near the cabanas," Angie said. "We'll grab a couple for you. What are you drinking?"

Get the hell out of the tub, I thought, *before I come, screaming, and embarrass myself!*

"Thanks," Bret said, "we'll get something in just a minute."

"Okay." Angie climbed out of the tub, followed, not quickly enough, by Frank.

As they walked away, Bret turned to me and rammed his cock into me beneath the water. With his fingers on my clit, I came, stifling my screams against his shoulder.

He silently filled me with his semen. "How did you do that?" I said a moment later when sanity returned. "You have a suit on."

"I discovered that the leg openings of these shorts are large enough for a quick exit if I need one."

"And you needed one. You were such a bastard." I would have swatted him, but I was so drained it was all I could do to talk.

"I guess I was, and eventually I got so horny I thought I'd go nuts."

"Well, it didn't show," I said, collapsing against the side of the tub.

"Thanks. I thought I sounded quite cool."

"You did. I'm impressed."

"Let's rest for a few moments, then find Frank and Angie. The night's still young."

Mr. Cameraman

*T*T ALL BEGAN WHEN MY HUSBAND, CHUCK, SIGNED UP TO take a course in film at our local college. One evening a week he enthusiastically drove off and returned filled with ideas. He was seldom without our digital video camera, and I was getting tired of being followed around by Mr. Cameraman with instructions. *Turn this way, move more into the light, don't look at the camera.*

He bought editing software for our computer and spent countless hours closeted with his machines. The second semester, he got lights and set them up at random times in random locations around the house. I would get home from work and he'd have already arranged his equipment in some spot so I could play some part.

I'm not complaining, mind you. He was happy and enjoying himself, and several times we'd rent a movie and he'd explain some of the techniques the pros had used. Finally, at the beginning of his third set of classes Chuck sat me down in the living room. "I'm going to make a real movie. I think I have many of the tools the real guys use and I've got a good idea for a plot."

"That's great. What can I do to help?"

"Jodi, you'll be the star."

"Me? You've got to be kidding. I don't even pretend to be able to act. I can't even lie to you with a straight face."

"There won't be too much acting, and the film will be short, maybe only a half hour. Please?"

Despite all my reservations I agreed. "Okay, I guess I'll do it, but don't blame me when I can't act. You said you had a plot. What kind of film is it going to be?"

"It's going to be a horror film, sort of like all those Jason movies."

I giggled. "Do I get to scream? Loud?"

"As loud as you want."

My laughter grew louder. "We'll have to alert all the neighbors so they don't call the cops. We don't want anyone dropping in or worrying."

"Okay, okay. You can take care of all those little details. I've got to work on my script." He hustled off to his workroom, and I didn't hear much more from him for almost a week. I called several people, all of whom found the idea just as hilarious as I had.

So filming began. The script was simple and Chuck assigned several of our neighbors and friends small parts. The scenes weren't shot in order, so it was a little difficult to keep track of what was happening, but we all kept our senses of humor and things went along just fine.

"Okay, Jodi, tonight's the big scene."

I had read the script and knew the climax of the film was to take place in our bedroom. The bad guy was going to break in and almost rape me. Actually it sounded kinky, but the film was going to be PG-rated so what could happen? "I've told you I don't want anyone in our bedroom filming anything like that."

"I know," Chuck said calmly, "and I've figured it all out. I've decided on an arrangement that will get it all done, privately."

"Okay, how?"

"Lex always does his dirty work wearing a stocking mask so I'll play the part for tonight." Lex was supposed to be a psychopathic killer who terrorized women.

"But Matt plays Lex in the movie."

"I know, but I'm about the same size as he is and I'll keep my face away from the camera just in case someone in the audience can make out anything through the stocking. I'll set the camera up on a tripod, pointing at the bed where the rape takes place."

"What about when Lex breaks in?" I asked, knowing the sequence of events.

"That will be a new technique I've come up with. The audience will just see darkness, with you on the bed. Sounds will tell the tale while you're sleeping. I've got it all thought through."

I wasn't sure Chuck could pull it off, but what the hell. "It's your film and if you think it will work, great."

"Wonderful," he said, brimming with expectation. "We can do it Saturday night."

"I'll be ready. As I remember the script all I have to do is scream and yell '*Don't*' a few times."

"I'm throwing away written lines for this scene. I think it will play more believably if you just do what you would do in real life."

"You mean I have to make up my own lines?" I didn't think that would work at all.

"Sure. And in case you get into real trouble at any point you can holler *uncle* and I'll stop. You know, if I kneel on you too hard or something. We've got to make it look real."

"I have one suggestion. I don't think we can do retakes as you've done in the past. I only have one of these in me."

"That shouldn't be a problem. The camera has two hours' worth of memory so I'll just keep filming and edit the final version."

On Saturday evening I dressed in a pair of baby-doll pajamas that Chuck had brought for the occasion. We'd loosened the seams so he could tear it if that seemed appropriate, but he'd guaranteed that nothing of my naked body would show in the ultimate movie. I certainly wasn't going to appear in a nude scene.

Fortunately there was a full moon that evening illuminating the bedroom with just the proper amount of light. I put on the outfit and looked at myself in the bathroom mirror. *Not bad,* I told myself. *Good figure, well-applied makeup, well-styled hair.*

When Chuck looked me over it was obvious he agreed. "You look great. I can't wait to rape you."

I laughed, but there was a little shard of nervous excitement inside me. I went into the bedroom and saw the camera angled at the bed. "Will it be able to pick us up with only the moonlight?"

"I bought a particularly sensitive one for just this scene. And if it works as well as I think it will I'll use it in my next opus. I've already got several ideas."

I climbed onto the bed and threw a sheet over me. Chuck arranged the fabric just so, then started the camera, turned out the lights and slipped from the room. I lay there, waiting for "Lex" to enter.

Moments later I heard the door creak ominously and felt a slight stir in the air. Suddenly a hand clamped over my mouth. "Scream and you're dead," Chuck said as Lex. He was dressed all in black, shirt, pants, shoes, socks and leather gloves, with a stocking mask over his face.

I tried to shiver for effect, but suddenly I slipped out of character.

I wasn't horrified at all, but rather excited by Chuck's dominance. I took a deep breath as he said, "If I take my hand off your mouth will you be quiet?"

I pulled myself together and nodded. Chuck slowly lifted his hand from my mouth. Soothingly and completely in character, he said, "That's a good girl." He grabbed my hands, pulled a piece of rope from his pocket and tied them to the headboard.

"Please, don't hurt me. If it's money you're after I can tell you where it is."

His gloved hands raked down my body, causing delicious tremors through me. "It's not money."

As my character I tried to remain afraid, but it was really difficult as Chuck positioned himself between me and the camera and ripped off my top. "So lovely," he said, then flipped the sheet back over me as was the trademark of the killer he was playing—and to keep the movie PG.

He climbed on top of me, straddling my sheet-covered thighs. He grabbed one ankle and efficiently tied it to the bedpost with another piece of cord from his pocket, then quickly did the same with the other.

"God, that's so sexy," he said, also slipping out of character. "Seeing you like that . . ." He cleared his throat and continued as Lex. "I'm going to use you to make your boyfriend the cop come over here."

"Don't," I said weakly. His hand raked my body. "Please." I was supposed to plead for my cop boyfriend's life, but I couldn't focus on the plot of the film.

"I'll do whatever I want," Chuck said. "And you can't do anything about it." He flipped the sheet away, and I could see from his smoldering gaze that the camera had been forgotten. "The moonlight on your breasts is just too tempting." He leaned over and sucked on nipple hard, causing me a mixture of pain and ecstasy. "Too tempting."

Then he used his teeth, sending shards of fierce pleasure through me. I had never dreamed that I'd like this sort of thing, but he was driving me to the apex of pleasure.

"I'd never thought about this kind of rough stuff, but it seems to suit you," he said, obviously knowing my state of arousal. "It suits me too." He grabbed the flesh of my thigh and squeezed, causing another shaft of desire. "Want to holler *uncle*?"

"No," I whispered.

"Good." He pulled off his gloves and with little difficulty ripped off my panties. He ran one finger through my slit. "So wet. This really gets to you."

I squirmed to try to show that I wanted to get away, but he wasn't fooled. "You're not getting away," he said, "and you don't really want to." He rammed one finger into me, causing my hips to buck. He finger fucked me for long minutes and yet my orgasm stayed just out of reach. "You're really into this," he growled, "and so am I."

He left me and stripped off his mask and clothes. In the bright moonlight I could see his erection, bold and hard. He saw me staring at him and grabbed his cock. "Want this?"

"Yes," I said, whimpering from need.

"Not yet. I want to look my fill at your helpless body."

The word *helpless* made my pussy muscles clench and my body jerk.

"You like that idea," he said, stroking his cock. "Being helpless, I mean." Watching me, he kept talking and stroking. "You're tied to the bed, wrists above your head, showing me your tits. Your ankles are tied, spreading your thighs for me, unable to press them together, unable to keep me out."

I closed my eyes and just listened as his words further inflamed me. "I'm going to fuck you now," he said, "ram my cock into you until you scream."

He crawled between my spread thighs and drove into me. I wanted to wrap my legs around him to force him deeper into me, but I couldn't. I just had to take whatever he wanted to give me.

He pulled out, then teased me with the tip of his erection, rubbing it over my flesh, then entering me with just an inch. He played with me, and I was unable to do anything about it. "Want to come?"

"God, yes," I moaned.

"Maybe I'm not ready."

"Please," I begged. "Please."

"I love to hear you begging for it." He rammed his cock home and, stretched out on top of me, pounded until we both came. My screams might have awakened the neighbors, but they had been forewarned about the movie. This wasn't acting, however. This was the best we'd had in a very long time.

We lay there, panting, for several minutes. Then Chuck said, "I don't know what came over me."

"Frankly, I don't care," I answered. "It was wonderful. I never would have thought . . ."

"Me neither. It just happened." He untied me, then turned to the tripod. "And we have it all on film."

"Oh, shit," I said. "I hope you'll destroy it immediately."

He leered in the moonlight. "Not a chance. I'm going to tie you to the bed one day soon and make you watch the spectacle you made of yourself."

"*I* made?" I said, horrified. "What about you?"

He kissed me. "Me too. If you want me to delete tonight from the camera's memory I will, but I think it would be dynamite to watch us. Like a porno film."

I thought about watching Chuck and myself. "I don't know."

He kissed me again. "How about we watch it next weekend and see what happens? Oh, and we have to film this scene again for the real film."

"I wonder whether we'll be able to play it straight or whether this will happen again."

"Do you care?"

I just purred. "Not at all."

Tammy's a Naughty Girl

❧

BEN PETROFSKY WORKED ON THE OPPOSITE SIDE OF THE office from my cubicle. We had seldom crossed paths until one hot Friday last summer. We had both been working late and when I finally closed and locked my desk and strode to the elevator, he was there, waiting for a down car. "Hi," he said, "I'm Ben."

I took a deep breath to calm myself. "Nice to meet you." He was kind of cute, with blue eyes, curly brown hair and a strength about him that was a turn-on for me. "I'm Tammy."

"I know. I've seen you around." The door to the elevator opened and he stepped in behind me. "Want to have a drink with me sometime?"

"Sure. When?"

"How about right now?"

"Okay." I certainly had no other plans.

We walked side by side to a small watering hole a block from work. Ben found us seats by the bar, where we sat sipping beers and talking about lots of things. Then he asked, "Did you hear that Carl hadn't done what they thought he'd done?"

I swallowed hard. "Yes, I heard."

Then he grabbed my wrist. "You're the one who started it all, aren't you?"

"I just told the truth."

"In the nastiest way possible, with the most hateful implications." He squeezed my wrist. "That was the meanest thing I've ever heard of."

"I didn't intend to be mean." The bastard was hurting my arm.

"I guess it's just a bad habit. There's a guy on the fourth floor who went to high school with you who says you've always been a bitch." He squeezed still tighter.

"Let go of my arm," I hissed. "You're hurting me."

"I think we need to go back to my place. You need a few lessons in manners."

Never one to make a scene, I said, softly but firmly, "Cut this out and let go!"

Throwing a few bills on the bar, Ben all but dragged me off the stool. "Be a good girl and don't make a fuss."

I hated to admit it to myself, but his attitude made me hot. Oh, I was angry at his high-handed antics, but no one had ever taken charge of me this way and it was very exciting. I glared at him but he didn't back down, nor did he let go of my wrist. "I'll scream."

"I don't think so." He stared into my eyes. "I think you've been looking for someone to take you in hand for a long time, and I'm just the guy to do it." He looked at my chest. "Your nippies are erect and I'll just bet your pussy's twitching up a storm."

I took in a breath to deny it, but it was true. My pussy was itchy and damp. "Get away from me." My protest sounded weak, even to my ears.

He moved his fingers to the inside of my wrist. "Your pulse is pounding and it's not from fear. You're hot for me and for what you know I can give you."

"I am not." Weaker.

His laugh was a combination of sexy and nasty. "My place is just a few blocks away. Let's go."

Did I have a choice? His grip on my wrist hadn't lessened a bit. I grabbed my purse as he all but dragged me out of the bar and around the corner. For several blocks I almost ran to keep up with him, until he turned into a three-story brownstone. He lived on the upper floor, and judging from the silence as we climbed the stairs, I could tell there was no one else in the building. "They're all away at the Tompkins' beach house for the weekend," he said. "We've got the entire place to ourselves."

He fumbled in his pocket for a key, then let us both into a comfortably furnished living room. He tossed me onto a sofa, and I rubbed my wrist, now red and sore. He flipped on the window air conditioner and pulled a beer from the small fridge. "One for me too," I said.

"Not a chance. You've been very bad and you need a few lessons in manners and the proper way to treat other people." He sat beside me on the sofa.

In a last burst of bravado, I got up and started for the door. "You've got to be crazy."

He whipped out his hand and grabbed me by the upper arm, flipping me onto his lap in one quick motion. He slammed his hand onto my butt. Although my flesh was well protected by my clothing, I felt the force of his blow. "You'll learn, and if I know my women, you'll like it very much." He pulled my skirt up to my waist in the back, exposing my white lacy panties. He rubbed the satiny fabric. "Nice."

I wanted to struggle, but the idea of getting a real spanking aroused me to new heights. When his hand fell on my ass, now covered by only one thin layer of nylon, I jumped, but I wouldn't give him the satisfaction of crying out. Again his hand fell.

"Let's see whether I'm right about all this," Ben said, pulling the crotch of my panties aside. He slid his fingers through my sopping wetness. "Oh, yeah, I was right. You're so wet you're about to come." He penetrated my pussy with his fingers, then pulled out. "Oh, you're going to learn a lot of lessons tonight."

He pulled my panties down until they lay around my ankles, and his hand fell a half dozen times on my bare butt. The heat of my rear flesh transferred to my pussy. I was on fire. He wet his fingers with my juices and slid a finger around my rear hole. I shot to climax and screamed.

His laugh was rich and full. "You're almost too easy. No challenge. Tell me that felt good."

I stared, but then lowered my head. I said nothing.

"From what I heard from the guy you went to school with you've been asking for this for years. Lucky for you I heard your begging." He stood me up, then washed his hands and got some lotion from the bathroom. When he returned he put me over his lap again and smoothed the cooling liquid over my heated butt. Actually the burning had stopped almost as soon as he stopped spanking me, but I whimpered, then *ahh*ed with pleasure as the cool salve and his caressing hand soothed me.

"Good girl," he said, "now you can do what I need." He unzipped his fly and pulled out his cock. "Suck it."

Now genuine tears began to flow. "I don't know how to give good head," I said in a very soft voice.

Again he laughed. "Well, now you're an honest woman. I'll show you. Pretend it's a peppermint stick and lick the length of it."

I did. The skin on his cock was soft like the skin on a peach. I inhaled his sexy fragrance as I licked. "Mmm," he purred and I was delighted. "Now pay some attention to the head. You don't have to take in into your mouth until you're ready. For now, lick it."

I used the flat of my tongue to massage the tip of his cock, then the point to tease the little hole. I thought he was going to fly right out of his chair. I took the first inch into my mouth and sucked slightly.

When he grabbed me by the back of my hair and pulled me away, I was miserable. Had I done something wrong? Quite the opposite. He came, gobs of goo flowing from the tip of his penis. I guess I did okay.

Eventually he regained his senses and said, "You're a very good girl and you learn very well. You will soon learn to be a better girl because you now know what you'll get if you're naughty."

"A spanking?"

"A very good spanking. Next time it will be with a paddle or a wooden spoon. So behave."

I grinned up at him. "Do I have to?"

His laugh was deep and rich. "No, of course you don't. If you behaved, I'd have divorced you long ago."

I climbed out of my character, one I'd played many times before in one guise or another. "You'd never do that," I said, planting a gigantic kiss on his cheek. "You enjoy our little scenarios too much."

He grabbed me and kissed me soundly. "You know I do."

Shave What?

❧

AUDREY GOLDMAN DIDN'T MIND THAT HER HUSBAND, Jack, surfed porn sites on the Internet. Actually it was a relief for her to be able to grade the stacks of essays and reports from her eighth-grade social studies classes and not feel that she was ignoring her husband of three years. The first evening he'd let his fingers wander they'd made really exciting and urgent love, and she found that she liked his newly adventurous side. "I get ideas from what I see, and I can't think of anyone I'd rather try them with but you," he'd told her.

Over the past few months he'd purchased several kinds of toys, which they'd played with on many evenings. More recently he'd discovered their mutual enjoyment of bondage so he'd bought a few pairs of handcuffs and two more exotic methods of restraining his wife. They both enjoyed that as well.

One evening Audrey finished the stack of papers she'd brought home and wandered into the den. She peered over her husband's shoulder and saw that he was gazing at a picture of a voluptuous woman. "She's nice," Audrey said, sounding a bit hesitant.

"Don't worry about your looks," Jack said. "I like you just the way you are, with one exception."

He tapped his finger on the monitor and Audrey saw what had sparked his interest. The woman had a completely bare pubic area. "I can't imagine why she does that," Audrey said.

"I think it's really hot looking," Jack said, and when Audrey glanced into his lap she saw that he was aroused by the sight. "Would you do that?"

"Not a chance. I've read in magazines about the itching when the hair grows back. It's fine for a day or two, but from then on it's nasty."

"If you kept it shaved it wouldn't grow back. I think it would be really sexy looking."

"You get that awful red rashy stuff, like the pimples that you get occasionally on your neck from shaving. Nope. Sorry."

"Okay," Jack said. "Just a thought."

"*You* could shave your cock and balls," she said, thinking that it might be easier for oral sex if his pubic area had no hair.

"Not when you make it sound so attractive." He shut down the computer. Later that evening they made love, but Audrey wondered whether Jack was thinking about the woman with the naked crotch.

After dinner a few days later Jack handed her a sheaf of papers. "Just in case you might reconsider, I printed out some stuff from the Net about shaving. The idea really excites me. Would you at least read this? I've read it all and there are lots of suggestions for avoiding the problems you told me about."

Since Jack was so interested, she'd go along at least this far. She spent the next hour reading all the pages Jack had printed out. The articles offered several good ideas for avoiding razor rash, as it was called, and lots of hints about the shaving itself. The problem of the stubble when the hair grew back was unavoidable, but it could be managed by either shaving often or just biting the bullet and letting it regrow. There were also products available that supposedly softened the new little hairs.

She thought about it. She loved her husband and really enjoyed it when he was aroused. This was something new and very different and if he really wanted it . . . "I guess we could give it a try," she told him that Sunday evening.

Her heart leaped when her husband's eyes lit up. "You mean it?"

She couldn't suppress her grin. He looked like a kid with a new toy. She knew she'd been right to do this, itch or no itch. "Sure." What was the worst that could happen? So she might be a little uncomfortable, but women did it every day. "Let's do it."

"You're going to shave?"

"No, you are going to shave me." She handed him the papers he'd printed for her.

She watched Jack's Adam's apple bob as he swallowed. "God, that's scary. What if I cut you?"

"It's your choice. If you want it done, you're going to have to do it for me."

"Okay," he said. "Let me reread some of this while you take a hot shower. We need everything really clean. And use some of that antibacterial soap."

Later in the bedroom as Audrey watched, Jack spread a plastic tablecloth on the bed and covered it with an old beach towel. He laid out a pair of scissors, a comb, a new disposable razor and a can of shaving foam. In the bathroom he filled a basin with hot water and added several face cloths.

As he reentered the room he said, "I can't believe you're doing this for me." He put the basin on the floor beside the bed and kissed his wife deeply. "You're really a treasure."

"Tell me that when the itching keeps me up all night."

"If it gets that bad, I promise I'll make it up to you." He patted the bed. "Lie down right here."

Audrey lay across the bed, her feet on the floor, her head on the pillow that Jack had set out for her. She parted her knees, exposing her most intimate parts to her husband. He leaned over and kissed her mound. "In a few minutes that should feel quite different."

In silence, Jack used the scissors to cut all of Audrey's pubic hair very short. Then he put a hot cloth over her mound to soften the hair that was left. "This isn't as easy as the web would make you believe," he said. "Someone on an online bulletin board suggested that an electric razor would do better on the inner thighs and the front of your mound. That way we'd only have to use an actual blade razor on the more intimate areas."

"Why is an electric better?" Audrey asked, trying to keep up casual conversation. She still felt really nervous.

"With an electric razor there's much less chance of razor rash." He went back into the bathroom and got his own electric shaver. "The downside is that it doesn't shave quite as close so the hair grows back more quickly."

Audrey's heart was pounding, both from her nervousness and from the arousal that her husband's playing with her body caused. "Whatever you say. You're the expert around here." Her hands grasped and released a handful of the sheet as she heard the buzzing of the shaver.

"Put your heels up near your butt," Jack said, "so I can get a better angle."

She felt his hands manipulating her pussy and tried not to think about it. She didn't want her flesh wet with her juices while he worked. She heard the buzz and felt Jack run the shaver over her inner thighs, then over her mound. When he was done he smoothed an antiseptic lotion over the newly bare areas.

He gazed at her now-hairless mound, then said, "Let me show you what I've done so far." He took a hand mirror and angled it so she could see what he'd accomplished. She gasped. Most of her pussy was bare. Nude. As she stared, so did Jack. "It's as sexy as I thought it would be," he said, caressing her smooth skin. "I can see your inner lips and your slit. Even with the little hair left it's soo hot. Maybe we don't have to go any further with the razor."

That would probably be best, and she had to admit that there was something daring about a naked pussy.

He laughed. "You're getting hot. I can see you swell, and the gleam of your juices is quite obvious." He stroked her mound, then slid his finger through her wetness. "You should see how incredibly erotic this is. Hang on—I've got an idea." He rummaged in the closet and found their video camera. "I can't get a mirror positioned for you so this will have to do." He connected the camera to the TV and switched it on. "Let me show you how you look."

She turned toward the TV and watched as the camera found her hairless mound. Jack held it at her feet, then zoomed in on her flesh until her pussy filled the screen. "Look at you. The sight of your cunt like this is getting to you. See the juices?"

Audrey could indeed see her wetness glistening in the light of the lamp. Jack put the camera down and got a goosenecked lamp from the computer room, plugged it in and positioned it so the bright light shown on her pussy. Then he turned the camera back on.

The heat from the lamp warmed her pubic area; the effect was deeply erotic. As she watched, her wet, swollen tissues filled the TV screen again.

"This is sort of an arousal detector," he said. "Let's see. I love your cunt and your nipples. I can watch your clit swell and pop out of its hiding place." He chuckled. "As I talk about it, it happens, and I can watch it all. You can't tell me that something doesn't get to you. Your body tells the truth."

He was right. She could feel herself get puffy and sopping wet. Jack knew how much she loved dirty talking, and he was very good at it.

"Now it's twitching. I can actually see it." He zoomed in on her clit, holding the camera with one hand and playing with her inner lips with the other. "This is amazing," he said. "My cock wants you right now, but this is too good."

She watched his fingers play with her, making her hot and hungry for him. "Let's do this all up right." He again put the camera down. "Don't move."

How could she? She was so hungry that her entire body was in flames, her brain unable to form a coherent thought. He returned with something in his hand, then picked up the camera again. With her cunt filling the TV screen he revealed a thick dildo from their toy bag. "Let's just watch this big boy disappear."

Oh God. She could see and feel him rubbing the head of the plastic cock over her hairless mound, then backward, slowly burying itself in her channel. She turned toward the TV and watched the phallus disappear into her newly visible opening. "Shit, baby, that's too much. You're going to make me come."

"Good. I want to watch you climax."

The combination of sensations was incredible. She could see herself, feel the dildo buried inside her, hear the whir of the camera and smell the unmistakable scent of her heat. She felt her body clench on the dildo as she came, a long, low groan escaping her.

Jack busied himself changing camera angles and zooming in and out as her body pulsed. Trembling, she started to come back down as Jack put the camera away and stripped off his clothing. Then he was inside her, obviously not as calm as his professional attitude might have indicated. "This is so sexy that I can't wait," he growled, thrusting and withdrawing until he finally poured semen into her.

Spent, the couple lay side by side. "That was amazing," Audrey said.

"Truly," Jack said, panting. "And we get to watch the film of tonight over and over too."

The thought of seeing it all again made her hands shake with expectation. "And next time I get to shave you."

"If that's half as hot as this was tonight, I can't wait."

She thought about what it would be like, shaving Jack's cock and balls, then showing him what he looked like with the video camera. The idea of watching his erection twitch with excitement made her lick her lips. Too bad they were both done for that evening. She'd have liked to try that right now, but the anticipation would be worth it.

"I've got to take another shower," she said, "to wash off all this activity." She winked. "I can't wait for our next 'movie of the day.'"

Dear Reader,

I hope you've enjoyed the stories in *Bawdy Bedtime Stories* so much that you want to read more of them. This is my fourth book of short stories, and I know you'll also enjoy *Bedtime Stories for Lovers*, *Naughty Bedtime Stories* and *Naughtier Bedtime Stories*. I have also written more than a dozen novels and more than eight nonfiction books about relationships and creating great sex with your partner. You can read about all my books, including excerpts from each, in the About My Books section of my website, www.joanelloyd.com. You'll also find lots more to enjoy there, including more than a hundred forums on dozens of varied sexual topics, tales sent in by visitors and a links page with hundreds of sites to visit. I encourage you to click over often as the material changes during the first week of each month.

I'd love to hear from you. Please drop me an e-mail at joan@joanelloyd.com or send snail mail to Joan Lloyd, PO Box 221, Yorktown Heights, NY. Just a warning: I don't get to answer my snail mail often, so please be patient. Got ideas for more short stories? I'm always writing, so please drop me a note about those too.

—Joan